THE UNICORN

≽ THE ≼
GATHERED
GLORY

Also by Bruce Coville

THE THIEF OF WORLDS
JEREMY THATCHER, DRAGON HATCHER
JENNIFER MURDLEY'S TOAD
GOBLINS IN THE CASTLE
ALIENS ATE MY HOMEWORK
MY TEACHER IS AN ALIEN
THE DRAGONSLAYERS
THE MONSTERS OF MORLEY MANOR
CURSED
SIXTH GRADE ALIEN

OTHER BOOKS IN THE UNICORN CHRONICLES

BOOK I: *Into the Land of the Unicorns*
BOOK II: *Song of the Wanderer*
BOOK III: *Enter the Whisperer*
BOOK IV: *Secret of the Delvers*
BOOK V: *The Invasion of Luster*
BOOK VI: *The Wounded Tree*

THE UNICORN CHRONICLES: BOOK VII

⇛ THE ⇚
GATHERED
GLORY

BRUCE COVILLE

SYRACUSE ❦ NY

THE GATHERED GLORY
Original copyright © 2010 by Bruce Coville
Revised edition copyright © 2022 by Bruce Coville

ISBN (paperback): 978-1-95532445-8
ISBN (hardcover): 978-1-95532446-5
ISBN (ebook): 978-1-95532447-2

All rights reserved.
No part of this book may be used or reproduced
in any manner whatsoever without written permission except in the case
of brief quotations embedded in critical articles and reviews.

THE GATHERED GLORY is a lightly revised and expanded version of the final third
of the book originally published as THE LAST HUNT by Scholastic Press in 2010.
It includes a new chapter written specifically for this edition.

Printed in the USA

First Scholastic edition: June 2010
First FCA Press edition: December 2022
2 4 6 8 9 7 5 3 1

Map by Katherine Coville

The text is set in Adobe Garamond Pro.
The display type is set in Ambrosia Caps.

Cover art © 2019 by Jerry Russell
www.JerryRussell.com

Series design standardization by Heather Wood
www.heatherwood.design

For information regarding permissions, write to:
FCA Press, 616 Westcott St., Syracuse, NY 13210

For
Nyxie Wednesday Coville
who lights up my life.

CONTENTS

Cast of Characters   1

Grimwold Speaks   7

CHAPTER 1
The Flame Sisters Talk   9

CHAPTER 2
Confusion   13

CHAPTER 3
The Creator   15

CHAPTER 4
A Bargaining Chip   20

CHAPTER 5
Rift   23

CHAPTER 6
Passing in the Night   32

CHAPTER 7
Signed, Sealed, and Delivered   37

CHAPTER 8
Seduction   43

DAY FIVE OF THE INVASION

CHAPTER 9
The Wizard in the Stone — 51

CHAPTER 10
The New Chiron — 59

CHAPTER 11
Namza's Last Dream — 66

CHAPTER 12
Battle Plans — 70

CHAPTER 13
The Creator Views His Creation — 76

CHAPTER 14
To Free a Wizard — 81

CHAPTER 15
Merry Fools, Desperate Task — 88

CHAPTER 16
Merging Magics — 95

CHAPTER 17
The Dragon and the Queen — 104

CHAPTER 18
Tunneling   109

CHAPTER 19
Convergence   121

CHAPTER 20
Enter the Players   132

CHAPTER 21
The Pieces of the Puzzle   140

CHAPTER 22
The Bloody Field   152

CHAPTER 23
Rajiv Steps In   159

CHAPTER 24
The Wrestling Match   166

CHAPTER 25
On Field of Battle   174

CHAPTER 26
To the Tree!   181

CHAPTER 27
Dragon Binding   189

CHAPTER 28
At the Center					192

CHAPTER 29
Transformations				205

CHAPTER 30
Fire Attend Thee				219

CHAPTER 31
Generations					221

AFTER
THE BATTLE

CHAPTER 32
Scars and Hope				229

Grimwold Speaks				241

Acknowledgments				243

About the Author				246

LUSTER
THE WORLD OF THE UNICORNS

Forest........ 🌳
River..........〰️
Swamp........
Hills..........
Mountains....
Water.........

Here There be Merfolk

AUTUMN-GROVE

0   25 mi.   50 mi.   75 mi.   100 mi.

CAST OF CHARACTERS

Following is a list of characters introduced in previous volumes of the Unicorn Chronicles. Characters who appear for the first time in this book are not included.

Allura: One of the Higher Powers, she occasionally appears in Luster for reasons unknown.

Alma Leonetti: As a girl, Alma found her way to Luster to ask the old Queen, Arabella Skydancer, to bring the unicorns back to Earth. This resulted in the formation of the Guardians of Memory. For her help over the years, Alma was granted a drink from the Queen's pool. As a result, she has aged very slowly. Though now quite elderly, she continues to advise the new Queen.

Amalia Flickerfoot: The new Queen of the Unicorns; as a youth Amalia was a restless wanderer much attracted to the human world, which is a dangerous place for unicorns. Hoping to keep Amalia safe should she ever be at risk of capture by Hunters, the Geomancer created a magic that would allow her to take human form. Using the magic caused Amalia to lose all memory of her life as a unicorn, and for decades she wandered in human form as Ivy Morris. She was finally restored to her true form when the previous Queen, Arabella Skydancer, departed this life.

Arianna: Granddaughter of the old Chiron (leader of the centaurs). She tended her grandfather until the time of his death. She loves a centaur named Arkon, who is the new Chiron.

THE GATHERED GLORY

Arkon: The new Chiron, a title he won by defeating his best friend, Basilokos, in fierce battle. The victory was tainted, because Basilokos was disabled by one of the quakes afflicting Luster.

Belle: One of the more fierce unicorns of Luster.

Beloved: The ancient and eternal enemy of the unicorns, Beloved seeks their destruction because of a horrible clash between her father and the unicorn Whiteling. Their struggle-to-the-death left the tip of Whiteling's horn lodged in Beloved's heart, where it both constantly wounds and constantly heals her. The horn has kept her alive for hundreds of years, but also keeps her in never-ending pain.

Cara Diana Hunter: Cara leaped into the world of the unicorns by using an amulet given to her by her grandmother, Ivy Morris (also known as "the Wanderer.")

Cloudmane: The first female unicorn to serve as a "Guardian Memory." Though she is often referred to as "gentle" she has a core as strong as steel.

Dimblethum (The): A large, slow moving creature who looks something like a bear who began to turn into a man but stopped halfway through the process. He is powerful and gruff, and not friendly with any unicorns save Lightfoot. He was the first to find Cara when she fell into Luster and is very protective of her.

Elihu: The object of Fallon's personal quest, Elihu helped Cara escape from being captured by the Hunters by making her transformation to a unicorn possible. He then disappeared as abruptly and mysteriously as he had first approached her.

CAST OF CHARACTERS

Fallon: Tall, muscular, with brown skin and long blonde hair, Fallon accompanied Ian on his quest to free Martha from the Rainbow Prison. But he is on a quest of his own, seeking his heart-brother, Elihu, who he believes may be found in Luster.

Feng Yuan: As an abandoned child in China, Feng Yuan was recruited to become one of the "Maidens of the Hunt" — young women trained to lure unicorns to their doom. After she saw the killing of a unicorn she left the Hunt. Due to her deep knowledge of Sun Tzu's book "The Art of War" she has become an advisor to the Queen.

Firethroat: Though ferocious by nature, this dragon is a friend to Cara, who once saved her from being controlled. In return, she granted Cara the gift of tongues, which lets her speak to all the creatures of Luster.

Gnurflax: King of the delvers, He is perpetually angry, and truly hates the unicorns.

Graumag: Smaller than Firethroat, Graumag was born as a human but became a dragon due to a spell cast by her wicked stepmother. When the dragons fled Earth, she did not thrive in the world where they went and nearly died. To save her, Bellenmore the Magician helped her come to Luster. She is the most sociable of the seven dragons.

Grimwold: An elderly dwarf who is the official Chronicle Keeper for Luster. He is responsible for recording new adventures and events after they happen.

THE GATHERED GLORY

Ian Hunter: Cara's father. He had worked for Beloved in the hope of finding Cara after she had been taken by her grandmother but later turned against Beloved. Ian occasionally loses his sight due to a desperate bargain he made to help him find his wife, Martha, and rescue her from the Rainbow Prison.

Jacques: An elderly and somewhat morose circus performer; he may or may not be Cara's grandfather.

Kenneth: One of Beloved's most trusted and faithful Hunters. He hates Ian, who he views as a traitor to the cause of destroying the unicorns.

Lightfoot: A rebellious unicorn prince who is next in line after the Queen to be leader of the unicorns. He finds this idea ridiculous, and is considered a bit of a disgrace to the royal family. He was the first unicorn Cara met after entering Luster, and the two have a strong friendship.

Martha Hunter: Cara's mother, recently freed from the Rainbow Prison by her husband, Ian. During her period of imprisonment no time had passed for her.

Medafil: A brave but slightly nervous gryphon with a strange speech pattern. He is a loyal friend to Cara — as he was to her grandmother in the days when she was known as the Wanderer.

Metzram: The king's wizard prior to Namza, and Namza's teacher. Though long since returned to the Stone, he lives on in Namza's memory.

CAST OF CHARACTERS

M'Gama (also known as "The Geomancer"): A tall, elegant woman of African descent, M'Gama's magic is worked through earth and stone. A trusted advisor to the Queen, she has been imprisoned in Delvharken, the underground realm of the delvers.

Moonheart: Amalia's brother and Lightfoot's uncle; he is a bit gruff and does not much approve of Lightfoot.

Namza: The king's wizard. Namza is worried by the influence the Whisperer has had on Gnurflax. Attempting to eavesdrop on the King and the Whisperer, he slipped into Stone while trying to avoid detection, and is now trapped there.

Rocky (Nedzik): A young delver who fears that Gnurflax has gone mad and is leading the delvers into great danger. The King declared him a traitor and stripped him of his name, one of the worst punishments that can be meted out to a delver. Cara gave him the nickname "Rocky" to help make up for this.

Rajiv: A street boy from Delhi who joined Ian's quest. He is undisciplined, but smart and intensely loyal to Ian and Fallon.

Squijum (The): A small, chittery, fast-moving creature who appears a bit like a cross between a squirrel and a monkey. He travels with Cara, and is mostly adorable, but also frequently annoying.

Thomas the Tinker: A kindly man who can mend almost anything, he is one of the most widely traveled humans in Luster.

THE GATHERED GLORY

Whisperer (The): A mysterious invisible being formed when the unicorns attempted a mass ceremony to purge themselves of all that was less than perfect. The coalesced form of all the hurts, jealousy, and anger that was drawn out of the unicorns, he is a tempter, a seducer, and a master of creating trouble and conflict.

GRIMWOLD SPEAKS

The time has come that here, in what remains of my cavern, I must take pen in hand to record the story of how Beloved's Long Hunt, which stretched across centuries as she sought the destruction of the unicorns, came to its conclusion. The joy and the sorrow, the triumph and the tragedy, that filled the last days of the Hunt must not be forgotten. It is my job to make sure the memory is preserved, for I am —

Grimwold

Fourth Keeper of the Unicorn Chronicles
The Queen's Forest, Luster

1

THE FLAME SISTERS TALK

Luster: Firethroat's Cave

Graumag felt a wave of apprehension as she approached Firethroat's cave. Other than a dragonmoot once every five years, the dragons of Luster did not usually visit each other. Territory was territory, after all, and not to be transgressed upon lightly. Still, she was glad it was Firethroat that the unicorn Queen had asked her to call upon; that venerable dragon was the closest thing Graumag had to a friend among the other six dragons who lived in Luster.

Though she never, these days, thought of herself as anything other than dragon, Graumag took some pleasure in this semi-friendship. There remained a human element of her heart that longed for companionship in the way that dragon hearts did not.

Once she reached Firethroat's mountain, Graumag flew back and forth in front of the cave, waiting to be invited in . . . though in truth she could not be sure that the lady was even at home. So she was relieved when at last a voice boomed out, calling, "What is it, Graumag? Why do you come uninvited to my lair?"

"Uninvited, but not unsent," replied Graumag. "Amalia Flickerfoot, Queen of the Unicorns, has asked me to speak to you."

"Then I guess I must hear what it is she has to say. You may approach."

This was not actually an invitation to enter, but it was a first step. Graumag threw back her head and blew out a gust of flame, as was proper. Then she dropped to the ledge that fronted Firethroat's cave. She perched there, her great tail dangling down, until Firethroat said, "How is it with you, Flame Sister?"

"I am affrighted by the quakes and tremors that are tearing at Luster. And you, Flame Sister?"

Firethroat scowled. "I, too, am gravely concerned." She paused, then said, "You may enter."

Graumag crawled into the cave. Even in the thin mountain air it was pleasantly warm due to the older dragon's presence. As always, Graumag was admiring of Firethroat's burnished red scales and in awe of her size.

The two beasts stared at each other for a time — it was never entirely comfortable for dragons to share a cave. Finally Firethroat stretched her head forward.

THE FLAME SISTERS TALK

Graumag did the same, and they pressed their necks against each other, the dragon version of an embrace.

"Though I do not often wish for visitors, I am glad you have come," said Firethroat, drawing her head back. "I have been sorely troubled these last days, for I have been in Luster hundreds of years and never felt anything like this." She cocked her head. "May I hope that you bring news?"

"I do, though, alas, it is not good. The woman Beloved has invaded Luster. To do so, she blasted an opening directly through the trunk of the Axis Mundi. That violation of the great tree is what has caused this troubling of the world."

Firethroat groaned. "I feared it must be something of this nature, but what you have told me exceeds my worst imaginings. Does the Queen wish us to fix the tree that holds the world together? That does not seem possible to me."

"No, she asks for help in another way. Beloved has brought with her nearly five hundred men trained to hunt and kill the unicorns. Amalia Flickerfoot has decided rather than wait passively for the end, she will go on the attack and she has challenged Beloved to meet on field of battle near the Axis Mundi. She wants to know if you will join her in this endeavor and fight on the side of the unicorns."

Firethroat smiled. "Now this part I actually consider good news! It is high time that the unicorns showed some fire and spirit . . . and long past time since I have had man to eat!"

Graumag winced a bit at this. Dragons had, mostly, given up eating humans some time ago. But, for Firethroat at least, the appetite had never entirely gone away. On the other claw, given what these men had come to do, she might be willing to feed a few of them to Firethroat herself!

2
CONFUSION

Luster: The Wilderness

Far away from the two dragons, the shaking of the ground — more violent now than ever — knocked the Dimblethum to his knees. The great creature groaned. It was not a groan of pain, or even fear, but of deepest despair.

What was happening to Luster?

He had been heading toward the great tree, which he somehow knew was where he belonged. But he had been moving slowly, deliberately. This was partly because of the wounds he had suffered in his battle to protect his friend Cara from a band of Hunters. It was also because he could no longer trust the ground beneath his feet to stay steady. But most of all it was because of the fog in his mind, which seemed more dense than ever.

At least he had heard no more from the wretched tempter who had whispered him into placing that sphere on the . . .

The Dimblethum's mind recoiled in horror. He had done something bad! Something very, *very* bad. But what? *What?*

He slapped at his bestial head, trying to dislodge the half-formed memory. Or perhaps simply to punish himself with some additional pain.

What had he done?

What had he done?

Beneath him, the world groaned and the ground rolled once again. Though he staggered, the Dimblethum managed to stay on his feet this time.

All this would be easier to bear if only there was something to fight. Why couldn't he find some delvers to crunch?

No! Delvers were not important right now. It was Luster that mattered.

He knew he had to get back to the great tree.

But why?

And why had he ever left it? He had always known that it was the most important thing in the world.

3

THE CREATOR

Luster: The Wilderness

Cara Diana Hunter, now in the shape of a unicorn and going by the name of Silverhoof, stared at Fallon. The big man's claim about the unicorns had struck her almost as powerfully as the energy from Elihu that had transformed her into a unicorn not that long before. Taking a few steps back so that she could look at him straight on, she whispered, "What do you mean, you created the unicorns?"

Fallon spread his hands as if the answer were simplicity itself. "I created the unicorns. They did not exist, and then I made the first pair. Pairs, actually. There were eight unicorns when I was done."

"Gaaah!" cried Medafil, who was standing behind Cara. "Did you create the gryphons, too?"

Fallon laughed. "It never would have occurred to me. Nor did I create you, friend Squijum," he added, nodding to the small, furry creature that was perched on Cara's neck, clinging to her mane.

Cara was glad for the interruption, since the jumble of questions pressing for her attention — "How? When? *Why?*" — seemed to clog her brain, making it almost impossible to speak. Finally she managed to whisper what seemed the most important of the three: "Why?"

Fallon was silent for a moment. Finally he said, "It's what we do, those of us at my level. But, really, why does anyone create? You feel a . . . a *restlessness* inside, a need to make something new, something no one has ever seen before. You want to add to the beauty and the richness of the world with a gift, an offering that is uniquely yours. It's an act of selfishness and generosity, all rolled into one."

Cara pondered this for a bit then said, "Does that mean you're the god of the unicorns?"

Fallon uttered a most ungodlike hoot of laughter. "No, it does not. And if it did, I would decline the position. I didn't make the unicorns out of a desire to control or to be worshipped. I made them . . ." He paused, as if searching for the right words, then finally said softly, "Creating them was an expression of joy. Joy and thanks. I wanted to give something wonderful to Earth, as a way of thanking that world for sheltering me after I was cast out of the Higher Realms."

"And how did you do it?"

Fallon shook his head. Smiling gently, he said, "That, my dear Silverhoof, would fall under the category of 'professional secrets.' "

Cara stamped a hoof in agitation. "Why did you tell me any of this if you're not going to explain?"

Fallon looked startled, then nodded and said, "I'm sorry. It's not that I want to be vague. But I've already explained more than I should. I would prefer not to invite additional punishment by spilling ancient secrets. I will say only this: I told you because *my* blood flows through your veins and because, though you and I are connected, there is something mysterious about you that I had hoped to learn in return. You are most clearly not just any unicorn."

Trying to sidestep his implied question, not ready to tell him of her human birth, she said, "If you made us, why haven't you been taking better care of us? We're in pretty big trouble, you know."

Fallon sighed. "You do have a gift for going straight to the heart of things, Silverhoof. Among the Powers, little is debated with greater ferocity than the question of what the creator owes the creation. Some feel you must hover over it, guarding it every moment. Others believe the highest, hardest, and most important task is to let go. They say that just as the parent must at some point release the child to the world, the creator must release the creation. Otherwise you stop it in its tracks, strangle its growth. Then you become not only the creator, but the executioner."

Cara did not answer right away. What Fallon was saying made sense, but at the same time troubled her, making her think of struggles she had had with her grandmother back on Earth, the fight between wanting to be independent and wanting to be taken care of. And the fact that Fallon was claiming, in a way, to be her own creator was far more than she could begin to think about at the moment.

"Now you, Silverhoof," said Fallon, his voice breaking into her thoughts. "I have told you my most treasured secrets. So, in fair trade, I ask: What is your secret? For I say it again: You are like no other unicorn."

Cara hesitated. Part of her ached to tell Fallon the truth about her heritage. Another part of her thought that to do so would be insanity. She had not known him long enough to trust him with her secret.

"How do I know what you told me is true?" she asked. This was no answer, but it did put the burden back on him, where she was glad to have it.

Fallon smiled ruefully. "I didn't expect my unicorns to be quite so cynical."

Probably you didn't expect any of them to have started life in human form, Cara thought.

Fallon shook his head. "Alas, what can I offer as proof? It's an ancient question, you know. For what do we require proof, and what must we take on faith?

I myself am not wildly faithful. In fact, I am a bit of a cynic when it comes to how worshipful those at my level are supposed feel toward the Powers above us. I suppose that's one reason I ended up in so much trouble." He smiled. "Maybe cynicism runs in the family. If so, I can hardly blame you for wanting more proof. But, truly, Silverhoof, I have nothing else to give you. Is what I have told you not enough to receive your secret in return?"

It was Cara's turn to sigh. How much proof did she require? Fallon claimed a connection to Elihu, who had made possible her transformation to her unicorn self. She could think of no test — what test could there be for such a claim? And she was weary of being alone.

Yet her own secret made her too vulnerable. She could not offer it to him.

"I'm sorry," she said softly, "I cannot tell you."

Fallon looked as if she had broken his heart. But he only nodded and said simply, "I hope someday you will trust me more."

With that, they resumed their journey toward the Gathered Glory.

4

A BARGAINING CHIP

Luster: The Stone Road

Ian Hunter was in considerable pain. This was due to the fact that the delvers who had captured him had bound him hand and foot, and he was now dangling upside down from a pole while two delvers in front and two delvers behind carried him along the stone highway.

Despite the pain, all he could think about was the fact that the delver horde was traveling in the direction he had sent Martha, Rajiv, and Lightfoot and he was wracked with fear that the little monsters might capture them, too. So his relief was considerable when, after another hour or so, his captors left the stone highway.

Even dangling upside down his sense of direction was good, so it didn't take long to realize that they were heading toward the Axis Mundi. His feelings were mixed. If they went to the great tree, it might prove easier for him to reconnect with Martha . . . assuming he could manage to escape. But it also meant the delvers might capture Martha and the others after all, since he had instructed them to return to the Axis Mundi the next day.

Accepting that he could do nothing about it until the delvers stopped for a time, Ian concentrated on staying calm, which was the only way he had of preserving his strength. The bonds chafed, and he felt a growing agony in his shoulders and hips. So he was relieved when King Gnurflax finally called for a rest and the team carrying the pole from which Ian hung suspended lowered him to the ground. He was still uncomfortable, and he had lost feeling in his hands and feet, but at least the pain began to ease.

The horde had been resting for perhaps an hour when a trio of delvers came trotting up. It didn't take long for Ian to discern that they were scouts, sent by Gnurflax to determine what lay ahead.

"We spotted a camp in the meadow southwest of the tree," said the first.

"Many tents, many men, many weapons," said the

second.

"We spied, sneakily, skillfully, and learned that it belongs to the woman Beloved," said the third.

Though their news was disturbing, it was Gnurflax's response that struck terror into Ian's heart. "Excellent news!" he crowed. "We have captured one of her men, who I am sure she would like to have returned. He will make an excellent bargaining chip." Turning to his commanders he said, "Rouse the horde! We continue our journey."

All too soon Ian was once again hoisted off the ground. With two delvers before him and two behind, sagging from the pole with his back occasionally scraping against the ground, he was carried toward the last place in either of two worlds that he wanted to find himself: Beloved's camp.

5
RIFT

Luster: The Stone Road

Lightfoot looked warily at Rajiv. The street boy stood in front of him with spread arms, his large, dark eyes filled with an urgent plea.

The three of them — Lightfoot, Rajiv, and Cara's mother — had stopped for a brief rest. It was their second day of trying to find the trail of the delvers who had abducted M'Gama, and the work had proved more tedious than Lightfoot would have guessed. It was made even harder by the worsening tremors, by his own growing sense of impending doom, and — in some ways worst of all — by Martha's desperation about finding Cara. Her barely contained terror only fed and fueled his own dark fears on that matter.

And now, again, the boy was asking to be brought into communication. As if to reinforce the request, Rajiv tapped himself urgently on the chest, then spread his arms once more. He looked both puzzled and hurt.

Martha moved to Lightfoot's side and put a hand on his shoulder. She took a deep breath, then thought to him, "Is there a reason not to let Rajiv communicate with you as I do? It would be easier for the three of us to talk if you did."

Lightfoot sighed. Why had he been resisting this?

Because I'm already connected with more humans than I ever wanted to be, was his first thought, which he was careful to shield from Martha. That felt true, but he knew there was more to it, so he pursued the idea. It wasn't, he quickly realized, just the number of connections. It was that the ones he had made already were so deep and intimate that they could be frightening and — in the case of Martha, who was filled with so much fear and anxiety — exhausting.

But the boy was sincere, and Ian had clearly thought highly of him, as had the strangely disturbing Fallon. And Martha was right, it would make things easier in their present circumstances. "Please step away," he thought to Martha. Then, wearily, he nodded his assent to Rajiv.

The boy returned a smile of such dazzling brightness that the Prince was almost glad he had decided to establish the connection. He lowered his head so that the tip of his horn was directly in front of Rajiv's chest, then pressed forward.

Rajiv had been prepared for the intense pain, but was surprised by how briefly it lasted, replaced almost instantly by a strange tingling that spread across his skin until he felt as if he had been kissed by a star. The feeling was disturbing, yet also warm and comforting.

The unicorn pulled back. Rajiv, slightly dazed, placed his hand over the bloodless wound, then bowed his head as a sign of thanks.

In response, Lightfoot extended his neck until the left side of his muzzle lay against Rajiv's cheek. Speaking mind-to-mind, he thought, "You don't have to use sign language now. You can communicate with me this way."

The unicorn's message came directly into the boy's consciousness as a mixture of images, sounds, and emotions that somehow carried a meaning even more clear than words. The sensation was so strange that Rajiv felt a brief desire to flee. But he held his ground and said, "Thank you, Prince."

"Do not speak out loud. You must *think* what you want to tell me."

Rajiv tried again. "Thank you, Prince."

"Much better. Now, why were you so eager for us to be able to talk?"

"Why would I not be? It is very hard to not be able to speak to someone you are traveling with."

He did not mention the envy he had felt of Martha and Ian for being able to communicate with the Prince, nor his simple longing to be in closer contact with this strange and beautiful creature. Nor did he ask why the Prince had resisted, something he was not sure he wanted to know. Instead, he added, "Besides, I am worried about the memsahib and thought we should speak about her."

"Why are you worried?"

"She seems as if she might . . . I don't know. Explode?"

Lightfoot chuckled grimly. "I know what you mean."

They both glanced at Martha, who had been pacing restlessly while they were having this conversation.

"But she has reason," continued the Prince. "She is worried about her daughter."

Rajiv was glad to know, from having listened to Martha and Ian discuss the matter, that while he could now communicate with Lightfoot, the unicorn could not simply read his mind. He did not want to reveal the depth of his own longing and loss when it came to parents.

At that moment Martha started toward them. Returning her hand to Lightfoot's shoulder, she thought, "We need to get moving again!"

"Most definitely," thought Rajiv, delighted to discover that the mind-to-mind communication could include all three of them at once.

* * *

Despite her gnawing fears, despite her concerns for her daughter and her husband, Martha Hunter felt alive in a way she had not for many years — not just the years of her captivity in the Rainbow Prison, but the years she had spent home alone while Ian trained for the Hunt and then, when that was done, went off in search of Cara. Now, at last, she was part of what was happening, no longer simply a passive bystander. With a frown, she corrected the thought. Not merely a bystander. When Beloved had cast her into the Rainbow Prison, she had become something worse: a victim. Now she had a sword strapped to her side, and a dagger in her boot, and she felt ready for a fight . . . in fact felt that she needed a fight.

But for now she had to focus on the more important, if less exciting, task of trying to find the trail.

She gazed ahead. The wide band of stone that she, Lightfoot, and Rajiv were following was obviously a natural formation. Even so, she could not help but think of it as a road. *The road to my daughter?* she wondered wistfully.

As they scanned the stone highway's edges for any sign of where the delvers might have veered off into the soft soil at the sides, she had to keep reminding herself that the search might be in vain, that their quarry might as easily have gone in the direction that Ian was now traveling.

She felt a deep urge to communicate with both of

her companions. From Lightfoot, she wanted to know more, much more, of his experiences with Cara. From Rajiv, she wanted details of his travels with Ian. But the intensity of their search for any sign of where the delvers might have passed made it difficult to talk. It was only when they were crossing from one side of the stone to the other to resume the search that there was really an opportunity. Frustratingly, those times were too brief for any serious conversation.

Despite her eagerness, her desperation, to spot something that might lead them to the underground world, Martha found it hard to maintain her focus on the task at hand. So much had happened in the last few days, and her mind was swirling with strange revelations clamoring for her attention.

She kept glancing at Lightfoot, trying to take in the fact that they were, to some degree, cousins.

The boy, Rajiv, was another matter. He was so down-to-earth in his approach to things that despite the fact that he was a homeless, parentless child her husband had taken from the streets of India, at the moment he seemed the most solid and grounded thing in her life. She was charmed by his courtesy and concern, and the way he addressed her as "memsahib." She sometimes found herself wondering if, when all this was over, she and Ian should try to adopt him. Whenever this thought arose she would immediately chastise herself for, yet again, letting her mind wander from the immediate goal.

Focus, Martha! she thought fiercely. *Focus!*

She wasn't sure how long they had been crisscrossing the stone road in their desperate search for any sign of the delvers' trail when Lightfoot suggested they take a break to eat.

Martha, who had her hand on the unicorn's shoulder at that moment, repeated this out loud for Rajiv.

"An excellent idea!" said the boy enthusiastically. "I am near to perishing from hunger!"

They had the food they had carried with them, of course, but Lightfoot showed them some other things they could eat. As it seemed wise to preserve their rations, they were more than happy to try them. Rajiv was particularly delighted by the root called *skug,* which looked unpromising with its wrinkled brown skin, but popped open to reveal a white interior that was crisp and tasty.

When they resumed their quest, Martha found it easier to focus and realized that hunger had been affecting her more than she had been willing to admit. Still, she looked up occasionally and was soon frowning as she saw how low the sun was growing. Before long they would have to stop for the night. They had agreed with Ian's plan that if they had not found the trail by the end of this day they would return to the great tree to await him. Even so, she found it hard to think of turning back.

She put her hand on Lightfoot's shoulder to discuss the matter and at once realized the Prince was also in deep distress.

"What is it?" she thought.

"I walk with fear as my companion."

Martha, who could think of many things to fear at that moment, replied simply, "Of what?"

"The death of my world. If Luster should fail — and how such a thing can be I do not understand, but it is clear that we are in danger of that happening — then what is to become of the unicorns? Many will die with the world, I know that. Even if some of us manage to escape to Earth, what then? That is no longer a place where unicorns would be . . . understood."

"It will help if you have friends with you," thought Martha, instantly trying to be comforting, which was a lifelong impulse. Then, because she could not stop herself, she thought, "My own fear is of not finding my daughter."

"I know. I see it in your every move and gesture, sense it in your every thought. But I tell you again, Cara is brave and strong and will surprise you with what she can do."

This calmed Martha, at least a bit. Even so, she thought, "I am not ready to stop the search and return to the tree."

Before Lightfoot could respond, she saw that Rajiv had joined them and motioned that it was all right for him to enter the conversation. As soon as the boy had put his hand on Lightfoot's other shoulder the unicorn thought, "Martha is not sure we should turn back tomorrow morning."

"But we told the sahib we would await him at the great tree!"

Martha, in contact with Lightfoot from the other side, could sense not only Rajiv's message, but the intensity of the boy's devotion to her husband, and was moved by it.

"Dark is drawing on," she thought to them. "We should wait till tomorrow to discuss this. Right now I want to continue the search as long as we still have light."

The others agreed. However, they had not gone on for more than five minutes when the strongest tremor yet rumbled through the stone, rocking and lifting it. Even worse, it did not cease, but grew in intensity, knocking all three of them to the ground.

"Memsahib!" cried the boy, scrambling ahead. "Follow me. This way! This way!"

Before Martha could respond, the stone highway split beneath her.

6

PASSING IN THE NIGHT

Luster: The Wilderness

Cara, Fallon, and Medafil traveled mostly in silence, each wrapped in his or her own thoughts. Even the Squijum was quiet for much of the time. Occasionally a tremor would cause them to cry out. More than once they fell against each other trying to get their footing.

Each time that happened, each time she brushed against Fallon, Cara felt that same odd thrill of recognition. Somewhat against her will, she found she was beginning to believe the big man's mad claim to have been the one who created the unicorns.

A few times, Cara asked Fallon to tell her about the Higher Powers, but he was unwilling to provide much information. Other times he was the questioner, asking about life among the unicorns. She remained equally vague, partly because she was annoyed at his own reluctance to speak, but more because she had not been in Luster — much less been a unicorn — long enough to answer most of his questions and so feared him catching her out. For that same reason, she dared not ask much about her father and mother, though the questions throbbed within her heart. It was enough, for now, to know that her parents were here in Luster.

As the hours passed, her sense of the unicorns grew stronger. She became certain it would not be long before she reached the Gathered Glory. Though she had been looking forward to that, she also felt a growing anxiety. What would she tell her grandmother when she finally saw her again?

Night fell. They continued to travel, coming to a broad stretch of stone that extended as far as they could see in either direction. Its surface was broken, and great gaps yawned where the tremors that shook Luster had pulled it asunder. They had traveled this road for perhaps an hour when Fallon placed a hand on her shoulder and whispered urgently, "Back up — step off the road."

She did as the big man ordered, moving in perfect silence. The Squijum, clinging to her shoulder, remained silent as well, as did Medafil.

A moment later she heard what had alerted Fallon: delver voices — a *lot* of delver voices. She wondered if the fact that Fallon had heard them first meant his ears were even more sensitive than hers.

Peering from their hiding place near the edge of the road, they watched as the delver horde flowed by. Cara tried to count them as they went past, but soon lost track. All she could be sure of was that there were hundreds of the little monsters. And what she did not see — could not see, because they were so thick upon the road — was that in the midst of them, carried at shoulder level, was a pole from which her father hung suspended.

"I take it those are the delvers you spoke of?" asked Fallon, once the horde was safely beyond them.

"Yes," whispered Cara. "Those are delvers."

"Never saw so many of the frat-spickled creatures in one place," muttered Medafil. "Kind of terrifying to see them all together like that."

"I wonder where they're heading," said Fallon.

"As near as I can make out, it's pretty much the same direction we're going," replied Cara nervously.

"Well, then, it looks as if everything will be decided at the center after all," said Fallon.

Medafil groaned.

Prompted by the sight of the delvers, Cara said, "I think maybe I should tell you where they came from."

Fallon looked at her quizzically.

"It has to do with the unicorns," she said.

"Then yes, I think you should tell me."

Wondering if she was doing the right thing, Cara unfolded the story she had learned from the Chiron, the story of how the unicorns had embarked on the ill-advised "Purification Ceremony" in which they tried to purge themselves of all imperfections . . . and how all the pride and envy and anger and hurt that had been pulled from them — very little in any one unicorn, but a great amount when merged together, and had led to the creation of the Whisperer.

Fallon listened in obvious dismay. "And you say that Elihu was part of all this?" he asked, his voice disbelieving.

"That's what the Chiron told me. But there's more."

Fallon groaned. "What else could there be?"

"The Whisperer, in turn, settled on a tribe of dwarfs, and corrupted them into the creatures you just saw going by. According to the Chiron, that's why the delvers hate the unicorns so much — because they were twisted out of their natural state by all the darkness that had come from the unicorns."

When Cara had finished speaking, Fallon turned away. She couldn't be sure, but she thought his shoulders trembled, as if he were suppressing a sob. She wondered if it was for the unicorns and their foolish pride, or because Elihu had been part of the dark event that led to the existence of not only the Whisperer, but also of the delvers.

After several minutes he turned back to her. His face was grim and hard, his eyes clear. But all he said was, "Thank you. This is something I needed to know."

"So it makes sense to you that this could have happened?"

As she asked the question, she realized she had been hoping he would tell her it was impossible.

"It makes all too much sense. And I fear it explains something that has been troubling me."

"What is that?"

But he merely shook his head and said, "Let us continue our journey."

"Secrets," muttered Medafil. "I hate secrets. Grukpingled things."

Cara felt the same way.

She would have been angrier about it were she not keeping a secret of her own from Fallon.

7

SIGNED, SEALED, AND DELIVERED

Luster: Beloved's Encampment

A cluster of delvers surrounded the bound form of Ian Hunter, who had been placed upon a long, low rock. Gnurflax, King of the delvers, leaned over his prisoner. Using a twig dipped in a pot of dark liquid, he scrawled some words across Ian's forehead.

Ian would have protested, but his captors had sealed his lips with a thick, foul-tasting paste, and he could not open his mouth.

"With regards from King Gnurflax," read the delver standing next to the King. "Beloved should like that," he added approvingly.

"Why do we wish to curry favor with the invader to begin with?" asked another of the delvers.

The King smacked him in the back of the head. "Because, you fool, she has one of the Queen's Five. She could not have entered Luster without it. I want that amulet so we can create our own passageway. And the best way to get it is to be friendly enough to find where it is hidden so we can steal it."

"As always, your wisdom exceeds all bounds," growled a third delver.

Gnurflax snorted, then said, "All right, the captive is ready. Take him to the woman's camp."

Ian did his best to ignore the hoots and catcalls that erupted from his former comrades as he was carried into Beloved's camp. He wanted to reserve his wits, and his strength, for whatever was to come next, and he couldn't afford to waste energy in reacting to mere mockery. His primary task now was to remain calm and hold himself ready for the smallest opportunity should it present itself.

Escorted by a group of Hunters, the delvers carried him directly to Beloved's pavilion. The gold and red tent, far larger than any of the others, was clearly the focal point of the encampment. Once there, they dropped him unceremoniously in front of the entrance, where Beloved's head man, Kenneth, along with another Hunter stood guard. Both men looked down at Ian with scorn.

"We wish to see Beloved," announced the lead delver. Since they spoke in delvish, the only word that could be understood was "Beloved." That was enough. Kenneth nodded and went into the tent.

A moment later Beloved emerged. She was dressed in a scarlet robe, and her moon-white hair swirled about her shoulders. When she saw the "gift" the delvers had brought for her, she cried out with malicious delight. Staring down at Ian, her eyes glittering, she said sweetly, "So, the prodigal has returned! You didn't really think you could get away from Grandmother Beloved, did you, Ian?"

When he said nothing, she bent and pinched his face between her fingers, puckering his mouth, which caused the delvers' paste to tear painfully at his lips.

"Poor Ian," she purred. "Captured by delvers, and now the cat has his tongue." Then, with a quick, sudden move, she slapped him. It was almost playful, yet hard enough to sting.

Rising, Beloved looked down at the delvers, who stood about waist high to her. She reached into the pocket of her robe and withdrew a stone. Ian guessed it was a speaking stone, similar to the one he had carried on his first trip to Luster. Her next words emerged from deep in her throat, sounding harsh and guttural. "To what do I owe the honor of this gift?" she asked in perfect delvish.

The lead delver bowed. Then, in grating tones, replied, "King Gnurflax sends this man as a reminder that the delvers are not to be toyed with. This Hunter made promises to the delvers that he did not keep." He kicked Ian in the side. "Thus do we deal with any who do not properly respect us. That the man lives at all is a sign of Gnurflax's mercy. The man is delivered to you as a sign of the King's desire to maintain good relations between us, since our people and yours are united as enemies of the wretched unicorns."

"This man has betrayed me as well," replied Beloved smoothly. "I have little use for him, save as a lesson to my other men that it is wisest to remain faithful. Still, I will accept him, as a mark of my ongoing friendship with the delver king. Should Gnurflax wish to speak with me about what is to come, I will be glad to host him and two of his closest in command."

The delver hesitated, then said, "Gnurflax wishes to know, lady, what has happened to so vex our world that it now shakes and quivers."

Beloved smiled, and in a voice close to a croon said, "Tell your King that Luster quakes at my power and that he should do so as well."

The delvers looked at her in terror.

"Now go!" she cried, flinging out a hand in dismissal.

The delvers turned and fled.

Once they were gone, Beloved crouched beside Ian. Staring into his eyes, she whispered, "I do not take betrayal lightly." Her voice was so soft that only he could hear her. "I poured a lot into you, Ian. Trust and love and training. Was simple loyalty too much to expect in return?"

With his lips still sealed by the delver paste, Ian could not have replied even if he had had anything to say.

Beloved sighed, as if his silence were one more betrayal.

"You could have had everything," she murmured. "Now, you will have nothing but a world of pain." Standing, she said contemptuously, "Take him inside, Kenneth. I will deal with him later."

As she strode away, Kenneth nodded to the other Hunter. Together, they lifted Ian's still-bound body and carried him into Beloved's pavilion, where they dumped him on the floor.

"Hard to have much sympathy for a traitor," said Kenneth, giving Ian a fierce kick in the same spot the delver had. The other Hunter simply spat on him. Then the two men turned and left the tent, leaving Ian bound and alone.

The world shook again.

Were it not for the fact that he could not, would not, surrender as long as there was the slightest chance of finding his daughter, of connecting again with his wife, Ian would have been just as happy for the ground to open and swallow him.

As if to make his misery complete, the Blind Man chose that moment to take his sight again.

He's welcome to it, thought Ian wearily. *It's a good time, actually, as there is nothing for me to see right now.*

In his blindness, he concentrated on trying to free himself from his bonds. But delver ropes are strong, and delver fingers are skilled, and he made no progress on loosening them.

Blind and bound, the best thing Ian could do was try to relax and save his strength. Who knew what chance might arise an hour from now? But even as he was trying to steady his breathing, he felt something new and unexpected and wildly frustrating. Beloved was summoning the Hunters.

It was an "all call" — something Ian could feel because even though he had rebelled, there still existed a bond between himself and Beloved. He knew that all the Hunters, no matter where they were, or what they were doing, would sense her command to return and begin making their way back to her.

For himself, being so close, the feeling was overwhelming. And it was flat-out maddening to be drawn to a woman he now so thoroughly loathed, even as the delver ropes held him bound in place.

But *why* was she calling her men back from the Hunt that she had so long desired?

What was she up to?

8
SEDUCTION

Luster: The Wilderness

As the road began to split Rajiv reversed course, lurching back toward Martha. Though she had flung herself forward, she had not been fast enough. Now more than half of her body dangled into the rift, the sword at her waist clanking against the rock wall. Stretching her arms, she scrabbled at the stone highway, desperately seeking any small hold to keep from slipping further toward certain doom.

And still the tremor intensified. The sound became deafening as the ground writhed and bucked and the gap in the stone grew ever wider. One twist flung Martha forward, but just as it looked as if she might be safe, the stone tipped up and she slid backward.

On the far side of Rajiv, Lightfoot was scrabbling desperately to get back to his feet.

Seeing Martha slipping backward, Rajiv threw himself flat and scuttled toward her. Screaming to be heard above the roar of the quake, he cried, "My hands, memsahib! Take my hands!"

Martha stretched for him and managed to grasp his wrists. The stone shivered again and she continued to slip back into the widening abyss, this time pulling the boy with her. "Rajiv, let go, *let go!* I don't want to pull you down with me!"

Ignoring her comment, the boy clung to her, shrieking, "Hang on, memsahib. HANG ON!"

Suddenly Lightfoot, legs splayed above Rajiv, snatched the back of the boy's shirt in his teeth. The muscles in his neck bulging, fighting desperately to keep his balance against the still-twisting stone, using every ounce of his strength, the unicorn halted their slide into the void.

"Hold on," he thought desperately, echoing Rajiv's plea to Martha. *"Hold on!"*

A moment later it was over. The stone ceased its tormented shaking and Rajiv, aided by Lightfoot, began to move back from the abyss, pulling Martha with him. They needed to raise her only a few more inches before she was able to pull herself back to safety. Flinging herself forward, she swept the boy into her arms and sobbed against his neck.

SEDUCTION

* * *

When they had caught their breath and gathered their wits, Martha, Rajiv, and Lightfoot stood gazing at the newly opened rift. The gap was several feet across — much too wide for the humans to jump — and it stretched as far as they could see in either direction, well beyond the edges of the road.

No point now in debating whether to go back to where they had first stepped onto the road. That route was closed to them.

"I hope we won't find another gap like this ahead of us," thought Lightfoot to the humans, who stood on either side of him with hands on his shoulders.

Which, as it turned out, was exactly what they did find only twenty minutes later.

"It's like being trapped on an island, Sahib Lightfoot," said Rajiv. "Only one with shores made of empty air instead of water."

Wearily, they turned from the impassable gap and moved into the surrounding forest. Rajiv, sensing Martha's despair took her hand and said gently, "I think we must follow the plan and return to the big tree, memsahib."

With a heart-deep sigh, Martha nodded and said, "Yes, Rajiv, you are right. Just pray that my husband has had more success than we have."

"I have great faith in the sahib," said Rajiv, all unaware that Ian was currently a prisoner of their enemy.

THE GATHERED GLORY

* * *

The forest floor was soft with the falling silver-blue leaves of autumn in Luster, so it was not hard to find a place to rest. Managing to fall asleep, however, was another matter altogether. It was difficult to relax when you feared that at any moment, and without warning, the ground might open beneath you and drop you into a dark emptiness.

So it was not surprising that Martha was still awake, staring morosely at the fat but waning moon as it shone through the branches, when a seductive voice whispered in her ear, "I know what you want."

Martha's eyes widened. "Who are you?" she whispered in terror. "*Where* are you?"

"Hush. Hush. I am someone who can make wishes come true."

The words were uttered in tones so sweetly soothing that Martha found her fear fading. Calmer, she asked, "What do you want of me?"

"It's not what I want that matters. It is what you want that concerns me. And I *know* what you want."

"How can you know that?"

"To me your heart is as an open book."

Martha shuddered and crossed her hands over her chest, as if to close that book. "Why can't I see you?"

"I am . . . a friend. You don't need to see me to know that. And I can help you, because I know what you want."

"I don't believe you!"

"You want your daughter "

Martha caught her breath, then said scornfully, "That doesn't take a genius."

"Maybe not. It might not take a genius to know where she is, either."

Martha sat bolt upright. "You *know* where Cara is? Will you take me to her?"

"Certainly. But you must understand that nothing is free. If I take you to her, I will need something from you in return."

"What?"

"Not much."

"*What?*"

"Why so distrustful?"

"I've had my fill of magic and have little reason to trust it."

"Do not be so cynical. You have no idea what wonders I can work."

"What is it you want?" she demanded.

"Just a little thing. Not much at all. Will you help me?"

"How can I answer unless you tell me what it is you want? I'm not so foolish as to agree to a blank check."

"Can you keep it between us?" asked the voice caressingly. "I would not like the others to know."

"Why? Will I be doing something wrong?"

"No, no! Of course not! Of course not. You will be a boundary breaker and a peacemaker. Think of how proud your husband will be."

"Please, just tell me what is it you want me to do."

"How would you feel about helping me to capture your mother?"

Silence.

"I know what she did to you."

"How can you know that?"

"I have my ways. I know many things that are hidden in human hearts."

"Why do you want to capture my mother?"

"You do not need to know that. You only need to know that I can lead you to your daughter."

"Will you hurt my mother?"

"Do you care?"

"Yes!" said Martha, surprising herself.

"Then I will not hurt her. Now will you help me capture her?"

Martha hesitated, then said slowly, "What must I do?"

DAY FIVE OF THE INVASION

THE AXIS MUNDI
Things fall apart; the center cannot hold . . .

—William Butler Yeats
"The Second Coming"

9

THE WIZARD IN THE STONE

Luster: Delvharken

When the shaking of the world had allowed M'Gama to escape the cell in which the delvers had imprisoned her, she had been surprised — and impressed — to discover that despite several days of shaking and destruction, the glowing orange lines that ran along the walls of Delvharken's tunnels were still working.

With the orange lines to light her way, she continued to follow her sense of the mysterious power that had been beckoning to her since her imprisonment began. She had no idea of how much time had passed when she heard a voice in the distance. It was the first sound, other than the groans of shifting stone, to reach her ears since the strange silence had descended on Delvharken. And it came from the same direction as the power she was seeking. She paused to pick up her chains so they would not clink against the stone. Then, moving more cautiously than before, she continued onward.

Rounding a corner she saw, several paces ahead of her, a lone delver crouched next to a lump of stone. The creature was wailing in despair.

M'Gama stepped forward cautiously. She did not particularly want to feel sympathy for a delver, but this one's distress was so obvious and so deep it was difficult not to.

Remembering that the language of the delvers was merely a warped version of dwarvish, and trying to recall how her captors had shaped their words, she said awkwardly, "What is it, delver? Why do you weep over that stone?"

The delver gasped — he clearly had not heard her approach — and drew away in fright. He stared at her for a moment, then cried, "I know who you are!"

M'Gama merely inclined her head, wondering at the dark, wavy lines that marked the delver's face. However, his next words caused her to gasp. Spreading his large, knobby hands, he said, "I am sorry about what happened to your servant, Flensa."

The Geomancer's immediate response was anger. Delvers had killed Flensa. Yet this one was apologizing. Why? Had he taken part in the attack on her home and now, facing her, begun to think better of it? If so, no mercy for that! After an uncomfortable silence she said stiffly, "How do you know what happened to Flensa?"

"Cara told me."

Now M'Gama was doubly startled. "You know Cara? You've seen her since she left my home?" Squatting so that her face was close to the delver's, she said, "We need to talk."

The delver nodded miserably, then drew an arm across his horribly upturned nose, wiping away the unpleasant result of his recent spasm of weeping.

Averting her gaze, M'Gama said, "Since you know who I am, why don't you begin by telling me your name?"

He gave a dark chuckle and said, "I have lost my name."

The Geomancer looked at him skeptically.

"King Gnurflax stripped it from me as punishment for treason," he said. Then, brightening, he added, "I do, however, have a nickname. In fact, it was a gift from Cara. She decided to call me Rocky and that is the name I go by now."

"Rocky will be fine," said M'Gama tartly. Despite this delver's seeming friendliness, she was not inclined to trust him too easily — nor to forgive him, whether he'd had anything to do with the attack on her home or not. From her point of view, all the delvers were equally blameworthy.

Another tremor shook the tunnel walls, causing

both Rocky and M'Gama to glance up in fear.

"Are those tremors why you were wailing just now?" the Geomancer asked.

Rocky shook his head, then looked around as if seeking some means of escape.

In the silence that followed, M'Gama realized that the strange power she had been sensing was close by. Yet she was certain it did not come from the delver she was talking to.

"Where have the others gone?" she demanded.

"They fled to the surface."

"Then why are you still here?"

Again Rocky glanced around. M'Gama wondered what he was looking for, then realized that he wanted to be sure there was no one near who could hear him. When he was satisfied that they were truly alone, he patted the stone he had been wailing over and said, "I was seeking this one."

The Geomancer was more puzzled than ever. "What one?"

Stroking the stone outcropping, he said mournfully, "*This* stone was once a delver. He was very important to me."

"A relative?"

"Closer than that. He was my teacher."

M'Gama was taken aback by the idea that this delver had had a teacher. Her sense of the creatures was continually being challenged. What else did she not know about them? Finally she said, "What happened to your teacher?"

Looking at her as if she were a slow child, Rocky said, "He turned to stone."

"You make it sound as if he did it to himself."

"Most likely he did. Few there are who could do it to him."

"He was powerful, then?"

The delver hesitated, then said, "Very."

"Can you think of why he would have done this to himself?"

Rocky was silent for a moment, then said slowly, "If he had been trying to hide, and tried too hard, it's possible this could have happened. There is a danger zone when you hover between flesh and stone. If you fall into it . . . well, I almost went there myself a while ago. I would have, if my cousins hadn't pulled me back." He paused, then added, "That's why you see these marks on my face. They are a sign that I have gone into the Stone and returned."

M'Gama took a moment to absorb this piece of information, realizing as she did that the delvers were far more complicated than she had suspected. "You say your teacher was powerful," she said at last. "Who could have frightened him enough to cause him to do this?"

"The King, perhaps."

"Did he fear the King?"

The delver burst out in a harsh laugh. "The King is a fool and a madman, and this one" — here he patted the stone again — "this one saw his madness and helped me to see it as well."

Stranger and stranger, thought M'Gama. Aloud, she said, "You claim you came down here seeking him. Why?"

"He is the wisest delver I know. The wisest delver there is, probably. The world is in great danger right now and we could use his wisdom."

As if to punctuate Rocky's statement, the tunnel walls shook again.

M'Gama leapt to her feet. "We can't stay here any longer. We should head for the surface."

"I can't go until I bring him back."

M'Gama looked at the delver in astonishment. "Bring him back? From being stone?"

"I told you, my cousins did the same for me."

"Yes, but you said you had *nearly* fallen into that state, not that you had become stone altogether."

"This one is much more powerful than I. It is possible he could become stone and still return."

Intrigued despite herself, M'Gama knelt beside Rocky. The chains that still dangled from her wrists clanked as she put her hands on the stone. "He *is* strong," she acknowledged. "I've been sensing him for days. Trying to figure out where that pulse of magic was coming from was driving me slightly mad." She hesitated, then added with a bit of wonder, "His power is much like mine."

"Of course it is. He is a Stone Wizard. You are the Geomancer. You draw your power from the same source. Please, *please.* You must help me bring him back!"

M'Gama's face hardened. "Bring back a delver? After what they did to Flensa?"

The delver bent forward and grabbed her feet. "You have to help! You understand these things. He is a stone magician. You are a stone magician. Call to him!"

And still M'Gama hesitated, as the part of her that had hated delvers for years struggled with the part of her that was seeing this delver not as an enemy but as . . . what?

Something almost human?

"I can get you jewels!"

M'Gama laughed, sounding crueler than she intended. "You cannot buy my help that way."

"Then what *do* you want, you horrible woman? I have helped your Prince Lightfoot! I have helped the girl Cara! I have sacrificed my name and my place in Delvharken to try to fight the King in his madness. What do you want? *Why are you so cruel?*"

He turned from her and flung himself back onto the stone, his shoulders wracked by fresh sobs.

M'Gama stepped back, startled. *Who is this creature to call* me *cruel?* she thought angrily. Then she caught herself. Closing her eyes, she took several deep breaths. As she gained control of her anger, as it lost its hold on her, allowing her to truly hear what the delver had been saying, the hardness in her heart began to melt. She took one more deep breath, then knelt beside the delver. "What must we do?"

He looked at her in shock. "You're the stone magician! Don't you know?"

M'Gama paused, then realized that she did, indeed, know what to do. The question was whether she could bring herself to do it. No, there were two questions. The first was whether she could sufficiently overcome her dislike of delvers to try this thing.

The second was whether she could find the courage.

10

THE NEW CHIRON

Luster: The Wilderness

The morning after Arkon the centaur had defeated his closest friend for the title of Chiron, he had galloped over the rim of the valley where his people lived and out into the larger world. Following him were fifty of the finest archers and sword-wielders the centaurs had to offer. Some of the band Arkon had chosen to accompany him had been his teachers; some had trained side by side with him when they were young together; and some he himself had taught the ways of sword and spear and arrow.

Each he would be willing to trust with his life. Yet

he mourned for the one centaur who was not among them, his old friend Basilokos, who had died during their fight for the chironate when a tremor had ripped open the ground beneath his front legs. His death had filled Arkon with a new sense of purpose.

Also driving him was the fact that Princess Arianna had already left the valley to attempt to find out what was happening to Luster. Arkon now accepted that, as she had argued, his duty lay beyond the valley's borders. But in the secret places of his heart he also hoped that in pursuing this duty he would find Arianna. She had left only a day ahead of them, after all. Yet now, at the start of their third day of hunting, he was beginning to despair. On an open plain you might spot someone from a distance, but in the deep forest you could pass within thirty paces of the one you sought and not realize he or she was there. There would be so many ways for them to miss her . . . especially if she did not want to be found.

He forced his thoughts back to the task at hand. *How do you find out what is causing a world to shake?* he asked himself. *That is a mystery never addressed in our training!*

The best plan seemed to be to seek out the unicorns. It was their world, after all. They ought to know something about this.

He was hoping Arianna had made a similar decision. With that in mind, he had gathered some of the maps collected by the old Chiron. Rolled tightly, they were now stowed in the quiver slung over his shoulder — a quiver that was, of course, also filled with arrows. . . .

The Chiron was jolted out of his thoughts by another tremor shaking the ground beneath his hooves.

"Arkon, look out!"

The call came from Danbos, the muscular centaur he had selected to be his second-in-command. The warning was well-timed. Though Arkon leaped the rift that had opened in the ground ahead of him nimbly enough once he saw it, without the call from Danbos he would likely have plunged in a foreleg. Glancing back, he shuddered, painfully reminded of what had happened to Basilikos and how dangerous the world had become. He would have to stay more alert.

The centaurs were crossing a broad grassland when Arkon spotted a pair of dragons in flight some way ahead of them.

"Look," he said to Danbos, who was cantering alongside him.

"That's strange," replied the other centaur. "I thought dragons were solitary beasts. Never heard of two of them traveling together!"

"There's a lot we don't know about this world," said Arkon bitterly. "I loved the old Chiron, but his letting the unicorns restrict us to our valley has left us in a state of ignorance. Worlds are for exploring, not hiding from."

As he spoke, the larger of the two dragons changed direction and started toward them. Did it want to talk

— or was it planning to attack? Because it was still some distance away, and because he did not want it to seem that the centaurs were afraid, Arkon continued forward. As they cantered across the grassland, it became clear that the dragons were farther off than he had thought — and, consequently, were also *bigger* than he had realized.

When the one approaching was close enough, Arkon raised an arm to halt his band. "Draw bows, but hold fire," he shouted. Alone, he trotted forward another fifty yards. Once he was far enough from the others, he spread his hands to show he was weaponless and it was safe if the dragon should want to parley.

"Tell your men to lower their weapons," called the dragon in a deep but clearly female voice. "We have no quarrel with each other."

"How can I be sure of that?"

"Because I have said so! Do you not know that dragons cannot lie?"

"How do I know that *that* is not a lie?"

"I cannot be responsible for your ignorance, centaur. I have information that may be of use to you. If you wish to speak with me civilly, I will impart it. Otherwise, I have my own work to do."

Arkon paused, then bowed stiffly from the waist and said, "I did not mean to be rude, friend dragon. Alas, we have not been much out in the world."

"It shows," replied the dragon tartly. "Now, shall we speak?"

Arkon turned and called, "Lower your bows."

THE NEW CHIRON

The centaurs did as he ordered.

The dragon, whose scales were the color of fresh blood, settled to the ground, sending small gusts of wind past Arkon. Coiling her tail around her — really, she was astonishingly large — she said, "My name is Firethroat."

"And I am Arkon."

"Good. May I ask, Arkon, why you have left your valley after all these centuries?"

"Is it not obvious? The world is crumbling beneath us. We seek to know the cause."

"That I can explain easily enough," replied Firethroat. Quickly she told the centaur what Beloved had done to the Axis Mundi, and how it was affecting Luster.

Arkon groaned. "Is there no hope for the world?"

"It seems unlikely. Still, if there is no hope, there may at least be vengeance! My companion and I are heading toward the meadow northeast of the Axis Mundi, to join the unicorns in their battle with the invaders, which is set for tomorrow morning."

"Then that is where we shall go as well," declared Arkon. He paused for a moment, then said, almost shyly, "In your flight, have you seen any other centaurs?"

"No, I have not. But to be honest, I have been more focused on my task than on watching below me. However your group was too large to miss."

Arkon sighed, then asked, "How far is it to the center?"

"If you mark the distance from your own valley, you have traveled about two thirds of the way."

"Then we shall be there by nightfall."

"I think I can speak for the unicorns when I say that you will be most welcome. I predict a day bathed in blood. If we do not live through it, at least we will have left our mark."

With that, Firethroat spread her batlike wings and took to the sky. She circled once above them, then called, "We will meet you at the center of the world. May it all be settled there." She shot forth a gout of flame as a kind of seal on the pledge, then turned to rejoin her companion.

Arkon watched as she flew back toward the other dragon. Only after the two of them were gone did he allow his hands a moment of trembling. He was no coward. Even so, it had been all he could do to control himself while face-to-face with the awesome beast.

He returned to his band and told them what he had learned. Then he consulted his maps — he spread them across Danbos's broad back to do so — and made a slight correction in their course.

Pointing, he called, "That way lies the center of the world. We meet the invaders there. If we cannot save Luster, we can at least exact a price upon those who have destroyed it. Are you with me?"

The centaurs roared their approval.

With their new Chiron in the lead, they galloped forward . . . not having any idea that Firethroat had directed them to the wrong meadow. She had not done that on purpose. After all, dragons cannot lie and that was where she herself believed the battle would take place.

But that was part of the Queen's plan. She needed Beloved to believe that place would be the site of battle . . . which would open the way for Amalia and the Gathered Glory to launch an unexpected attack on her actual camp. She regretted not letting Firethroat know her true plan, and expected she might pay a price for that deception. But she had had no choice. It was vital that the dragons believe the battle would be in that meadow. Otherwise, not being able to lie, they could not pass that false information along to Beloved.

11

NAMZA'S LAST DREAM

Luster: Delvharken

Namza, still trapped in Stone and therefore unaware of the conversation between M'Gama and Rocky, once more began to dream.

The dream this time was of what had happened the night he had bid farewell to his own teacher, Metzram. As he drifted into that memory, Namza saw himself as he had been back then, still young, filled with uncertainty, and his heart breaking at the thought of losing his teacher.

As clearly as if he was actually living the moment again, he felt himself kneel beside Metzram, who lay on a stone pallet, shivering under a coarsely woven blanket.

"It will not be long now, my student," Metzram whispered, reaching out to take Namza's hand. "Soon I must return to the Stone from which I came." His voice was feeble. His breathing sounded like pebbles rattling in a tube.

"Do not go, Teacher! I am not ready to take your place."

"Nor was I when the time came for me to let go of my own teacher," came the quavering response. "We are never ready, young Namza. We simply do what we can. And what we must." Hit by a sudden spasm of coughing, he tightened his grip on his student's hand. When the fit had passed, he said, "Namza. Student. Friend. Life is harder for you and me than it is for others, for we know things the others don't, things it is not yet safe to tell them."

Namza nodded, knowing that to speak what they had learned, what they now understood to be the source of the delvers' anger, and that it was possible for them to be "softer" could cost them their lives.

"It's not just the danger," Metzram wheezed, as if he had read his student's mind. "The greater fear is that if we do speak these things too soon, tell the true source of our ongoing anger, the denial will be so strong that the truth will be lost altogether. And it must not be lost! The changes we need to bring must come, but they can only come slowly, as slowly as the change that comes to stone when water wears against it, making its shape something new."

Metzram coughed again. The terrible sound struck fear into Namza's heart. The older delver smiled wanly and whispered, "Not long now."

"Teacher, stay with me!"

"I am ready, Namza. I —"

Metzram's eyes widened as he saw something — clearly something unexpected — behind his student. Puzzled, Namza turned to see what could have drawn the dying delver's attention. He gasped. Standing near the entrance of the cave was a beautiful woman, with skin as brown as *zakram* leather and hair as yellow as the dreaded sun. He knew at once it must be the woman his teacher had told him of.

"Lady Allura!" gasped Metzram. "You came!"

"I owe you that much," said the woman who was, from a delver's point of view, absurdly tall. She walked to the stone pallet where the old delver lay, knelt on the side opposite Namza, and placed her hand upon Metzram's high, domed forehead.

"Your touch is cool, lady."

"It is meant to soothe," replied Allura.

"It does," murmured Metzram.

"The time of transition draws near, venerable one."

"I know," he replied, heaving a sigh that changed to a sharp, shuddering gasp.

"Teacher!" cried Namza.

But the moment had come. Metzram's body stiffened. The flesh began to gray. Then the cracks appeared, signifying that he had returned to the Stone.

Namza wailed and lay his head upon the breast of his teacher, which was now solid rock.

He wept for so long that he was surprised, when he raised his head once more, to see that the woman was still there.

"There is another story you need to know, young delver," she said softly. "I do not know when, but I am certain that the time will come when someone must bear witness. The tale I want to tell you is not in the pages your teacher stole for me so long ago. Rather, it is etched in my heart. Will you listen to me tell it? Will you remember the story and hold it in your own heart until the time is right?"

If Namza could have shifted in his sleep he would have, for he knew what was coming. But he could not move, any more than he could stop the dream. Yet a moment later the dream ended, anyway, interrupted before Allura could tell her story.

Someone was calling him through the Stone.

Who was it? What did they want?

Namza resisted. Sleep was good. Dreaming was good.

But the voice would not let him be, insisting that he wake and respond.

12

BATTLE PLANS

Luster: On the Route to the Axis Mundi

Amalia Flickerfoot gazed out on the Gathered Glory with a mixture of pride and terror. Standing beside her was the strange Chinese girl, Feng Yuan, who had unexpectedly become her guide to the art of war.

That her gentle people were now ready to fight for their home was a source of inspiration to her . . . and also of grief. Her heart was pierced by the blood-certainty that many of them would be dead before the night was over. What made it hurt even more was that she knew her unicorns did not really understand war and its horrible toll. Despite the Long Hunt, their

BATTLE PLANS

deaths had been scattered, random. Not having spent decades as a human, as she had, meant they had never experienced anything like what was going to happen this night.

Of course, that was assuming Luster even lasted until nightfall. She had begun to fear that the plans she had worked out with Feng Yuan and Belle were pointless. What if Beloved had accomplished her goal of destroying the unicorns simply by entering this world? How much more of this quaking and shaking could Luster endure before it just fell apart?

Feng Yuan placed a hand on her side. "You seem troubled, My Queen," thought the girl.

"How could I not be troubled, given what we face this night?"

"Let us call together your leaders and review the plans one more time. It may ease your spirits."

As the Queen's Council was gathering, a unicorn — one Amalia did not know by sight, though that was not unusual now that the unicorns had converged from all corners of Luster — came trotting up and said, "We have a visitor."

"Thank you, um . . ."

Not knowing his name, she let the sentence hang. After a moment the messenger ducked his head and said shyly, "My name is Seeker. I believe you knew my second cousin, Finder."

The Queen felt another lance of sorrow. "He was very dear to me, Seeker. Now, who is this visitor?"

"A centaur, My Queen. She does not speak our language, but I was able to determine that her name is Arianna and that she wishes to meet you."

"How did she find us?"

"She didn't. One of the outrunners found her."

Feng Yuan, who had remained in contact with Amalia through this conversation, smiled. The outrunners, or scouts, had been her suggestion.

"Bring her to me, please."

"As you wish."

It was not long before the centaur was standing before them. Her horse's body was larger than that of all but the biggest unicorns; her human portion, rising from the front shoulders, added more height, with the effect that she towered over the Queen. She spoke a few words, but they were incomprehensible to Amalia.

"That sounds like a form of Greek," Feng Yuan told the Queen. "I know only a bit of it, and what I did learn is differently spoken from what she has said. Even so, I may be able to communicate with her enough to explain how she can be opened to mind speech."

"Go ahead and try," replied Amalia.

Feng Yuan began a halting conversation, carried on partly in broken Greek, partly in sign language, that finally led to Arianna nodding and spreading her arms. At this invitation Amalia stretched her neck and, straining upward, pierced the centaur's chest. After a brief cry of surprise, Arianna smiled. She bent at the place where her human form flowed into her horse aspect. Then, following Feng Yuan's example, she placed her hand upon Amalia's neck. As with most, it took a few tries before the Princess grew accustomed to speaking mind-to-mind, but she got the knack of it soon enough.

"What brings you to our camp?" asked the Queen.

"I was traveling toward the Axis Mundi, eager to learn what is troubling the world, when one of your people spotted me. I had been hoping to find the unicorns, thinking you might know what has disturbed Luster. So I was happy to follow him to your side."

Amalia quickly explained to the Princess what Beloved had done to the Axis Mundi, then said, "We are about to discuss plans for our final confrontation with the enemy. Do you wish to fight at our side?"

"With all my heart! I have met your granddaughter, you know. She did something . . . difficult for us."

"She has told me of it," said the Queen. "I was proud of her, and I offer you my condolences on your loss."

Arianna nodded. "In granting my ancestor's deepest wish, Cara earned my eternal gratitude. It would be my honor to fight at her grandmother's side."

"I am happy to have you join us. From what I know of centaurs, you are somewhat more warlike than we, and so may have much to contribute."

Feng Yuan agreed, despite the flash of jealousy she felt at this statement.

The council had been gathering while the Queen and the Princess spoke. Now Moonheart stepped forward and said, "Let us begin our meeting."

"Agreed, brother," said the Queen. "Let us begin."

The plan was simple, really, and relied largely on their hope that Beloved, believing them to be brutish, would not think them capable of the deception they were now plotting.

"Let me understand," said Arianna at one point. "Beloved believes you will meet her in the field northeast of the tree tomorrow morning. But you plan instead a surprise attack on her own camp this very night?"

"That's the basic idea," replied Feng Yuan.

"It will help," added the Queen, "if Beloved is aware that dragons cannot lie."

Arianna wrinkled her brow. "Why will that help?"

"Because I sent a dragon to deliver this challenge."

"I'm confused. If a dragon cannot lie, how could it deliver a false challenge?"

The Queen grimaced. "Because I lied to the dragon. She will be annoyed with me when she finds out. I am not looking forward to telling her. It is far better to stay in a dragon's good graces."

"Are the dragons with you now?"

"Nearby. They will join us later in the evening, which is when I will tell them. It will be on their signal that we attack. We do not have a bugler to announce the charge and do not want to provide such a warning, anyway. Instead the dragons will be positioned at either end of our flanks. When the time comes, they will shoot two columns of flame into the air. That will be the signal for the charge."

"And how will they know when to do this?" asked

BATTLE PLANS

Arianna, intrigued by what the unicorns had planned.

"We have arranged for a diversion in the camp," said Feng Yuan with a smile. "When the Hunters are sufficiently distracted, two humans, members of a group called The Queen's Players, will alert Graumag and Firethroat that it is time. And then . . ."

"Yes?" asked Arianna.

The Queen's face was grim. "Then we end the Hunt forever — or die trying."

13

THE CREATOR VIEWS HIS CREATION

Luster: The Wilderness

Fallon was fascinated, and slightly troubled, by his new companions. Not so much the gryphon and the chattery little creature; unusual beasts were well within his range of experience, though something about the Squijum seemed oddly familiar. No, it was the unicorn, Silverhoof — there was something strange about her that he could not identify. She knew so much about some things and so little about others. And that bit of Elihu he sensed in her — her claim of having simply met him once was not enough to explain that!

THE CREATOR VIEWS HIS CREATION

Of course, he was well aware that there were things she was not telling him, sometimes under the guise of not knowing them, though she was not very good at deception. But most of his confusion came from what he felt when they were in contact. Even as he sensed the connection of blood and magic he had with all unicorns, with her the feeling was muddled somehow, as if there was something else inside her. He might have thought it was simply a sign of how unicorns had changed in the centuries since he had last been in contact with them, save that he had felt no such oddness from Prince Lightfoot. He could not figure out what it meant, and it was maddening.

Despite that, Silverhoof was the least of his concerns. It was the strange tale she had told about the Whisperer that occupied most of his thoughts. Could Elihu really have done something so mad as to assist at that Purification Ceremony? Fallon sighed as he forced himself to admit that doing this was of a piece with his *alahim's* other actions.

And how might he have been punished for this act of hubris? That was the soul-twisting question. It was possible the Higher Powers might not have noticed and thus would not have interceded. But Fallon's instincts told him this was highly unlikely.

He sighed.

"What troubles you?" asked Silverhoof.

Fallon shook his head, then smiled. "That is usually my question. It is rare for someone to feel concern on my behalf."

The unicorn looked at him curiously. "Don't you have friends?"

Her words pierced him, and he thought for a time before saying, "I have people I have helped. They would consider themselves friends, and I have a strong fondness for many of them. But my path is, mostly, a solitary one."

"You need to relax," said the unicorn.

Fallon actually laughed.

"What?"

"As I said, I am usually the one who tries to help. I'm just not used to such concern. Or such bluntness. It is most welcome."

"I see," said the unicorn. Then she asked a question that completely startled him. "What are you going to do about the Whisperer?"

"Why do you ask that?"

She shook her mane in irritation. "Because you've been brooding ever since I told you the story. Because I watched your jaw clench and your hands tighten as I was telling it. Because for some reason, I can tell that the idea of it really got under your skin. So, are you going to fight him? It? Whatever?"

Fallon stopped in his tracks. Several moments passed before he said, "Yes, I think I'm going to have to. Though I don't know that 'fight' is the right word. But it definitely requires a confrontation."

He started to say something else, but stopped, his heart lifting with an unexpected joy at what he sensed ahead of them.

THE CREATOR VIEWS HIS CREATION

"What is it?" asked Cara.

"Unicorns," whispered Fallon. "Hundreds of them! Not far from here."

"It must be the Gathered Glory," Cara replied eagerly. "They're heading for the Axis Mundi to do battle with Beloved."

"How do you know that?" asked Fallon.

"A dragon told me."

"Silverhoof, you continue to amaze me. And given how old I am, and how much I have seen, that is no small thing. What do you think — shall we join them or stay separate for now?"

Cara felt an unanticipated burst of shyness. How well did the unicorns know one another? Could she simply lose herself in the Gathered Glory, or would she be taken to her grandmother? Certainly Fallon would be expected to meet the Queen if he were to try to join them. The likelihood was that she, Cara, would be taken along with him. If so, what would she do then?

"I don't know," she said nervously.

To her surprise, Fallon said, "Neither do I. Perhaps we should simply observe for a bit."

"Gad-fingle it!" said Medafil, shaking his wings. "What are you two afraid of?"

"Caution is not the same thing as fear, friend gryphon," replied Fallon gently.

"Well, fear or caution, I intend to go to the Queen."

"I'd rather you didn't just yet," said Fallon.

"Actually, Medafil, I don't think I'm ready to join them, either," said Cara.

"Stig-fraggle it, what's wrong with . . . oh!" He stopped his sputtering and turned his eagle's head to stare at Cara with one gleaming black eye. She could tell he realized she was uncertain about what to tell her grandmother. "All right," he sighed. "I'll stay with the two of you."

"Not two, *many!*" complained the Squijum, which actually made Fallon laugh.

They began to move in a loop, circling around the unicorns. At one point they mounted a low rise where they could, by standing behind a row of dense bushes, look down and see the Gathered Glory, which gleamed among the trees. Cara could hardly bear the longing, the urge to rush down and become part of that great and beautiful wave. She turned to Fallon to say that maybe it was time after all and saw that he had fallen to his knees. Tears were streaming down his face.

"I didn't know," he murmured after a moment. "I just didn't know . . . "

"Let's move on," said Cara softly, feeling an unexpected tenderness for the man. "Since they're heading toward the Axis Mundi we can join them there if we want."

In this, of course, Cara was mistaken. Her grandmother had no intention of going to the Axis Mundi at this time. The Queen's plan involved heading for somewhere close to it, but far more dangerous.

14

TO FREE A WIZARD

Luster: Delvharken

"Do you have a knife?" asked M'Gama.

Rocky looked at her, puzzled. "What for?"

"Never mind what for! Do you have one? If not, help me find a sharp stone."

Without another word, she began searching for such a stone herself. The dim glow of the orange lines that ran along the corridor was sufficient for her eyes, which were long accustomed to low light. As she searched, she realized something that she had previously noticed, but that hadn't completely registered because she had been focused on so many other things: The delver tunnels were beautifully crafted. She would have found no sharp edges, or even any loose stones, if the tremors had not done so much damage. As it was, she crossed to a pile of rubble where part of the ceiling had collapsed and quickly located a shard about a foot long. Running a finger over it, she murmured, "Perfect."

Returning to the outcropping over which she had found Rocky weeping, the Geomancer knelt in front of it. She held out her left arm and drew the edge of the shard across her flesh. Blood welled out, scarlet against her ebony skin. She turned her arm so the blood could drip onto the stone outcropping, then closed her hand into a fist and clenched it. She repeated the action, the blood flow increasing each time she did. When she was satisfied that she had enough, she relaxed her fingers. Then she used her right hand to pinch the divided flesh together, chanting in a low voice until the wound had sealed itself shut. It was not healed, and would not be for some time, but the bleeding had ceased.

She took a deep breath, then placed her hands upon the bloodied stone. Turning to Rocky, who stood watching nearby, she said, "What is his name?" When the delver hesitated, she snapped, "If you want me to bring him back, I need his name! His *true* name. You must know that much."

Rocky swallowed hard, then whispered, "He is called Namza."

"Ah," said M'Gama. "The King's wizard."

Rocky nodded.

M'Gama closed her eyes and pressed her forehead to

the stone. She began to chant in a low voice, *"Amma kreymos petra. Amma kreymos petra vivat!"*

She felt the stone open to her, felt her magic begin to weave its way between its very atoms.

Hear me, O Namza, she thought. *Hear me! I am M'Gama, the Geomancer, and I have come to call you back from Stone.*

No answer.

Hear me, O Namza, she thought again, more fiercely this time. *If you are still here, if there is any part of you left that can answer, then I bid you do so. I have sensed your power for days now, and it is akin to my own. Though you are delver and I am human, we have much in common. Wake, O Namza! Wake from this stony sleep and return to your living shape. Your student has need of you. I have need of you. Lus . . .* Delvharken *has need of you.*

No answer.

The tunnel walls shivered around them once more, but M'Gama did not notice. Again she called, and yet again, forcing her voice, her mind, her very self, into the Stone.

At last she sighed and began to withdraw in defeat. But as she did, she felt something stir. In her head a voice — faint, as if from a great distance, but clear nonetheless — whispered, *Wait. I will come with you.*

Rocky watched in horror as the Geomancer gasped and rolled off the stone she had been trying to call back to life. She now seemed lifeless herself. Scrambling to her side, the delver pressed his ear to her chest. To his relief, she was still breathing. Before he could check on her further, a new sound caught his attention. He looked back, then cried out in joy.

Namza was returning from the Stone!

With a lunge, Rocky threw himself against the outcropping that had once been his teacher. He remembered, too well, the terrible cold he had experienced as he returned from his own near-Stone experience. Because Namza was older, and had gone much deeper, he feared the old wizard would be that much the worse upon reviving.

M'Gama groaned behind him, but Rocky's focus was entirely on his teacher now. Slowly, very slowly, as if some invisible sculptor were carving him, Namza was returning to delver form. First a broad outline appeared, crude shapes that might be seen as arms and legs, as a delverling sometimes imagines he sees the shapes of delvers in the walls of a cave. Heartbeat by heartbeat the lines grew deeper, the shape more distinct, until it was obviously a delver. Just a delver, though — any delver, not one with a name and a personality. Yet on the process went, the features becoming ever more pronounced, the brow high, the chin wide, the age lines deep, until at last it was clearly Namza and no other.

Then, as silent, clear, and swift as when the moon emerges from behind a cloud, came the moment when

Namza's form shifted from stone to flesh and he lay shivering in his pupil's arms.

Rocky held the old wizard close, muttering soothing words and feeling strange that he was now doing the comforting, after all the times his teacher had comforted him. Gazing at his teacher, Rocky realized there was one significant change — to the age lines that had long marked Namza's face had been added the kind of dark, wavy lines that now tattooed his own face — the lines that marked someone who had gone into the Stone and somehow been brought back.

"Dear student," whispered Namza, lifting a trembling hand. "Is that you?"

"It is I, Master. I have come for you."

"But who was it that brought me back? It was a great power that called me, a great power indeed."

"It was M'Gama, the Geomancer," replied Rocky, feeling regret and shame that he had not been able to work the magic himself.

"Is she well? She put forth a mighty effort."

Rocky turned to glance at M'Gama and stifled a cry. The Geomancer remained still and unmoving upon the tunnel floor. "I must check on her. Will you be all right?"

"The cold is fierce," said Namza, still shivering. "But it will pass. Look to the lady."

Scuttling back across the stone floor, Rocky knelt beside M'Gama and asked urgently, "Lady, are you well?"

She moaned and her eyes fluttered open. "Not yet," she whispered. "But I will be. I simply need to rest."

As if to contradict her words, to say there was no time for rest, the walls of the tunnel shivered and they heard stones falling somewhere behind them.

"What was that?" cried Namza in alarm. "What is happening to Delvharken?"

"The world is wounded," replied M'Gama, her voice still weak.

"How can this be?" gasped Namza.

"Delver, help me to your teacher's side," said the Geomancer. She pushed herself to her knees. Leaning on Rocky, but not rising to her feet, she knee-walked across the stone floor, her chains clanking as she went. When she reached Namza she looked at the old wizard, shook her head as if she could not believe what she was about to do, then leaned forward and pressed her brow to his. Then she began to communicate, wizard-to-wizard.

After a few moments Namza cried out in fresh horror. "This is what I have feared! How long do you think we have before it is too late?"

"A day, two at the most," replied M'Gama. "After that, this world, Luster or Delvharken, whichever you choose to call it, will shake itself to pieces."

Namza groaned. "Is there no way to heal the tree?"

"None that I know of."

"That is why I came searching for you, teacher," whispered Rocky. "I hoped *you* would have the answer."

Namza closed his eyes. "I wish I had as much faith in myself as you have in me, my student."

Even as he spoke the world shook again, causing a boulder to crash down just feet away.

"We must get out!" cried Rocky. "We must go to the surface!"

Before M'Gama and Namza could struggle to their feet, another tremor rippled through the walls of their tunnel. With a roar, most of the ceiling collapsed, boulders thundering down on either side of them.

15

MERRY FOOLS, DESPERATE TASK

Luster: Sweetwater

After an arduous journey, most of it underground, Grimwold finally reached the village of Sweetwater. He was both annoyed and relieved to find that his calculations about where to find Armando and the Queen's Players had been correct. Relieved because he knew that this was what the Queen wanted. Annoyed because . . . well, this was going to be bouncier than he liked, and ridiculously exuberant.

He heard them before he actually reached the village, of course. This was no surprise. They were, after all, a noisy lot.

With a sigh, he hurried forward . . . and was amazed, when he reached the place where the Players were encamped, to see that there was a unicorn standing beside one of their wagons.

The moment he stepped into the clearing where they were gathered, a dozen Players joyfully cried "Grimwold!" Three of the men grabbed instruments — a flute, a trumpet, and a drum, which Grimwold considered an absurd combination — and played a minor fanfare.

Four brightly colored wagons were arrayed around the clearing. The back door of the largest flew open and out sprang a short, chubby man. He managed to ignore the steps attached to the back of the wagon by simply bounding over them. Landing deftly on his feet, he took another leap forward, did three somersaults, and ended up standing, with a broad smile on his face, directly in front of Grimwold.

"Greetings!" he cried merrily. "Greetings, O Chronicle Keeper, Master of Stories and therefore Source of Inspiration. Armando de la Quintano and The Queen's Players welcome you!"

"Greetings, Armando," replied Grimwold, somewhat wearily. "I'm glad to find you here."

Before Armando could reply a tremor shook the ground, knocking Grimwold onto his back. Armando, aided by decades of circus training, managed to keep his balance — though just barely.

Grimwold got back to his feet, muttering curses

under his breath as he did. Once he was steady, Armando said gently, "Where else would we be, my friend? Have we not visited this lovely village at this time for many years now?"

At that point the unicorn who had been standing beside one of the wagons came to join them. Grimwold studied her for a moment, then said, "Ah, Cloudmane. It is lovely to see you again . . . though also a considerable surprise to find you in this place!"

"She carried me here, at the Queen's request," said a familiar voice. Turning toward the speaker, the Chronicle Keeper saw two men step down from the leftmost of the four wagons. The face of the one who had spoken was worn and weary. This was Jacques, and every time Grimwold saw him, he thought how odd it was that despite his dour face and slumped shoulders, the aging tumbler carried more jokes and riddles in his brain than there were stories in the Unicorn Chronicles.

The other man — bald, snub-nosed, and dressed in an absurdly colorful patchwork coat — was Thomas the Tinker. He appeared equally serious, which was unusual, since Grimwold knew, from many previous meetings, that he was normally as cheerful as Jacques was solemn.

But then, these were not normal times.

"Greetings, my friends," said the Chronicle Keeper. Then, speaking specifically to Thomas, he asked, "Have you succeeded in the task the Queen set you?"

"I have," replied Thomas, with a slight shudder.

"I'm impressed. After Amalia told me what she had asked of you I did not expect I would ever see you again — or at least not see you both alive and successful, since it seemed your quest must end in either death or failure!"

"Thomas is a continuing source of amazement," said Armando happily. "He really should have been an actor!"

This led to another fanfare and a round of cheers from the Players. Nine of them built a human pyramid in Thomas's honor. When they finally calmed down, Jacques said to Grimwold, "Can we assume that you bring new instructions from my former bride?"

Grimwold winced. Jacques had, briefly, been married to Amalia Flickerfoot during the time that she was trapped in human form as Ivy Morris. As a result of that long ago situation, he hoped himself to be Cara's grandfather. But the Queen had never confirmed that, and Jacques had not yet found the courage to ask her flat out.

"I do indeed bear a message," said Grimwold. "The Gathered Glory is traveling to the center of the world to do battle to the death with Beloved and the Hunters. The Queen asks her Players to join her and the unicorns of Luster in this mighty effort."

An odd smile creased Jacques' face, pulling up at the deep-edged lines. Turning to Armando he said, "Well, old friend, the time has come at last. Are you ready to perform for the enemy?"

Armando turned to the Players, who were gathered

in a half circle around them. They were a motley crew, arrayed in everything from rags to spangles, but alive with joyful energy. "You heard the message," he cried. "Are you ready for what we have discussed?"

The response was a mixture of cheers, headstands, flips, and drumrolls.

With a grin, Armando said, "I do believe we are ready."

"As are we," put in a new voice.

With those words, Hiram Lewis, the unofficial headman of Sweetwater, stepped into the clearing. He was followed by nearly twenty men of varying ages. Though not armed with swords or shields, each carried one of the tools of his farmwork: a pitchfork, a hoe, a rake, a pick, or an ax. Though meant for helping crops grow and thrive, it was easy to see how these things could be used to take life as well as help nourish it.

Cloudmane edged closer to Jacques, who put his hand on her shoulder. He was silent for a moment, then said, "Cloudmane asks me to thank the men of Sweetwater, and assure you that the Queen will be most glad of your assistance."

Hiram Smith, gray-bearded and sturdy looking despite his age, replied, "It has been our privilege to live here in peace and safety for the many generations since our forefathers first stumbled into Luster. To assist in this battle is the least we can do in return for the shelter granted us, and I believe I can speak for the other humans in Luster when I say that if there were time to gather them, they would gladly join us in this effort as well."

At that moment another tremor, worse than the previous one, shook the clearing. When it was over, a grim-faced Hiram concluded, "This may be the last thing we ever do. Luster may fall, but until it does, we stand with the unicorns!"

"As do we all!" shouted the Players.

"As do we all," murmured Grimwold. Then he added, "And may the Higher Powers grant us strength as we do."

When the men had dispersed to make their final arrangements, Cloudmane thought to Jacques, "My work here is done, and I wish to take word to the Queen that all is in order."

"How in the world will you be able to find her?" asked Jacques. "I mean, we know where she is headed, but . . . "

"The more unicorns that are gathered in one place, the easier it is for me to sense them," replied Cloudmane. "The Gathered Glory is the greatest assemblage of unicorns in my lifetime, and the pull toward them that I feel is so strong it has taken a mighty effort of will to stay here with you this long. Now I should go."

"Thank you for bringing me here," replied Jacques. "May we meet again on the other side of this."

"May we meet again," answered Cloudmane, and

if there was an edge of doubt or fear in her thoughts, Jacques did not comment on it.

She turned and galloped away. Jacques sighed as he watched her go, and thought once more, "May we meet again."

Then he went to join the others as they worked on refining their plans for the battle to come.

16

MERGING MAGICS

Luster: Delvharken

Namza, who was very old and very wise — though perhaps not as wise as his student liked to think — had been terrified when the tunnel roof collapsed. Such fear was a sensation he had not felt in more years than he could remember. But for all his long life he had believed Delvharken unshakable. In the few moments since he had returned from the Stonesleep, that belief had been shattered like a rock beneath a delver's hammer.

The orange lines had finally failed, making the darkness complete. Even had the lines still been glowing, the air was filled with so much dust from the collapse of the ceiling that they would likely have appeared as no more than dim orange smears.

Where were Nedzik and M'Gama? Had they survived the stonefall? Namza tried to call out, but the choking dust made it hard to breathe, and he began to cough instead.

From nearby, a shaky voice said, "Teacher, is that you?"

Relief flooded Namza's heart. His student, at least, was still alive. With that thought came a question: How had Nedzik found him down here to begin with? The old delver scowled. He wasn't supposed to call the boy by his real name anymore. On the other hand, what was that cruel ruling but additional proof of Gnurflax's tyranny? Not only that, it was his — Namza's — fault the lad was such a rebel to begin with. The old wizard corrected himself. No, it was not his fault; it was his success! If nothing else, he had taught the boy to think for himself!

"Teacher?"

"Yes, I'm here and unhurt. But what of the Geomancer? M'Gama, are you with us?"

"I'm here," she called, then began to cough from the effort.

"Well, we all survived," grunted Namza. "That's one thing. Now all we have to do is find a way out."

He sounded more positive than he felt.

"Any ideas?" asked M'Gama.

Namza tried to read her voice, seeking tones of

challenge or despair. But she had kept it marvelously neutral. He was impressed.

"Well," he replied, "the first thing we need is light. Can you call it from stone?"

"Not unless I know the stone. Can you?"

"With the same limitation. Which means we'll have to start by learning the stone that surrounds us." He hesitated, then said, "It will be faster if we work together."

Silence.

"Come," he said sharply, "do not be shy. Our magics have already touched and mingled or you could not have called me back to begin with."

The Geomancer's reply was indirect. "Why are you so different from other delvers?"

"Age has its benefits."

"This is not a time for jesting! You are not like the others and I want to know why."

Namza sighed. "If that is what is required for your cooperation then I agree to tell you." Thinking of his recent dreams, he added, "Indeed, I believe you will find it interesting when I do. But surely there will be a better time for such a tale!"

"True enough," said the Geomancer grudgingly. "All right, how do you suggest we begin?"

"Let us join hands. This will be easier if we are in contact."

Namza heard M'Gama moving toward him. A moment later her outstretched right hand grazed the back of his head, causing the chain that dangled from her wrist to knock against him.

"We should start by getting rid of these chains," Namza said. "Give me your other hand as well, please."

M'Gama did as he asked. Once their hands were firmly linked she heard him murmur a few words. To her surprise, the clamps that held the chains to her wrists parted. She shook her hands, and the chains fell away.

"How did you do that?" she asked.

He chuckled. "Well, I made them to begin with, so it was easy enough to undo the spell that held them. I used to do that sort of minor magic for the king. He always took it for a greater thing than it was, which left me free to work on other, more important things. Now, let us join hands again and enter the Stone."

He could feel the Geomancer's magic twine around his as they moved their power into the Stone. Another tremor rippled through Delvharken. If he still had a mouth, he would have cried out in agony, since now that he was in the Stone it was as if his own body was being twisted and torn by the shifting rocks.

Once the tremor passed, M'Gama thought to him, *I did not expect that to be so painful. Nor did I expect our powers to merge so easily.*

Perhaps we are not as different as you have wanted to believe, replied Namza.

When the Geomancer did not respond to this, Namza felt a brief flash of anger, then reminded himself that delvers were prickly as well. Perhaps he was expecting too much of her. Opening his mind, he thought, *I am ready to work.*

As am I.

Their first task was to learn the stone surrounding them. This proved to be fairly simple, partly because the stone here was basic, partly because their magics were combining more easily than either of them had anticipated. Once they had studied the form and structure of the stone and examined a bit of its history, Namza thought, *Ready?*

Ready.

Together they began to coax out the energy hidden within the stone, teasing it loose, freeing it. Slowly at first, then at an increasing pace, the stone began to warm around them.

"The walls are beginning to shine!" cried Rocky.

By common consent, and without speaking a word, Namza and M'Gama set the magic so it would hold, then retreated to their bodies. When they opened their eyes, it was to a space permeated by a soft glow, though the light came as if through a fog because of the choking dust that still filled the air.

"The light should last long enough for us to find a way out," said Namza.

"Or make one," replied the Geomancer.

"That will require merging magics again," said Namza.

M'Gama closed her eyes, then said, "I am ready to

do that, ancient one. But if we manage to live through this, when it is over I will expect you to answer my questions." She paused for a moment, then added, "I think there are things we can teach each other."

"Of that I have no doubt," replied Namza. "I have long wished that you and I could be in contact, for I agree there is much to be learned. But now is not the time for that discussion. Let us try to find a way out while we have light. If that does not work, we can try to move, if not mountains, at least a few stones."

His words proved prophetic; several minutes of searching showed the space in which they were trapped to be sealed on all sides.

"Well," Namza said glumly, "it appears that shifting some stone is our only option."

"The problem is," said M'Gama, "we don't know where to start. There's no point in trying to burrow our way through a tunnel clogged for a half mile ahead of us."

"Then we must return to the Stone to find the best place to do this," said Namza.

Now that they had twice merged magics, reentering the stone was easily accomplished. Finding the best place to work, however, was difficult, and the answer, once located, was distressing.

That barrier is almost impossibly thick, thought M'Gama in despair.

It would be easier if we could attack it from both sides, Namza replied.

MERGING MAGICS

Yes, and if stone were made of sugar we could just eat our way through.

Tut! Are you always so gloomy?

This is hardly a situation to inspire mirth, replied the Geomancer, as another tremor shook the rock around them. *If you have a suggestion, just tell me.*

I do. Let us return to our bodies, and I will explain.

A few minutes later M'Gama was looking at Namza with astonishment and new respect. "You can really do this thing?"

The stone wizard patted his left shoulder. Realizing the Geomancer might not recognize the sign of affirmation, he said, "Yes, I can. It is not easy, nor is it done without pain. But it seems the best tactic at the moment. I spotted a tiny channel through the stone. As you correctly noted, if we place one of us on each side of the barrier it will be easier to open a complete passage."

"Teacher!" cried Rocky. "You know this will pain you!"

"So will dying before my time, though I suppose if I attempt this, that is one possible result. Now be still and let me concentrate."

The dusty air was still illumined by the spells they had placed in the stone walls, allowing M'Gama to watch in admiration as the old wizard began a magic she knew was possible, but had never dared attempt herself. He sat crosslegged on the cave floor. Resting his hands on his knees and closing his eyes, he began to chant. The Geomancer followed as much of the magic as she could, but too many of the words were unknown to her. She would not be able to repeat this spell — not that she was likely to want to try!

An acrid odor permeated their small space. Soon after that, Namza's skin began to grow scales. His body trembled with the pain of the coming transformation. He moaned, then loosed a horrible cry of agony as he began to shrink.

Rocky clapped his hands to his ears and threw himself facedown.

The old wizard's robes sank in, then collapsed.

A moment later, a small brown lizard wriggled out of one sleeve. It looked at M'Gama, flicked out its tongue, then scampered up the wall and disappeared into a tiny crack.

Trying to ignore the pain that had accompanied his transformation, Namza entered the thumb-wide opening he had spotted when he and M'Gama had been exploring the stonefall from inside.

"Be careful, teacher!" his pupil called from behind him.

Namza did not reply, mostly because being careful would have prevented someone of his age from trying this to begin with. As he scurried though the tiny opening, he hoped he had been correct that it extended all the way to the other side of the stonefall, no matter how far that might be. He also hoped, even more intensely, that the world would not shift again until he had made it through.

In this latter hope he was disappointed. He had crawled about ten feet along the narrow opening when a low rumble set his tiny heart racing with terror.

The stone was moving again.

He knew that not far ahead was a larger space — a kind of pocket in the stone at least five inches across.

Namza scrabbled toward it as fast as he could, hoping to reach it before the walls closed around him and smashed his tiny body to a lizardly pulp.

17

THE DRAGON AND THE QUEEN

Luster: The Gathered Glory

Amalia flinched when young Seeker brought word that Firethroat had been spotted heading in their direction. In order to explain the next part of the plan that she and Feng Yuan had concocted, she was going to have to confess to the dragon that she had deceived her when she asked her to carry that challenge to Beloved.

She was not at all sure she would survive the moment. Firethroat could be reasoned with when she was calm, but according to stories Amalia had heard from the time she was a mere foal, the dragon's temper was awesome when aroused.

THE DRAGON AND THE QUEEN

Feng Yuan, who was standing next to her, placed a hand on her shoulder and thought, "Whatever happens, I will stay by your side, my Queen."

Amalia resisted the urge to reply, "You'd better, since this was mostly your idea!" She held back, partly because it had, in truth, been a good idea, and partly because she knew that it would have been her human side speaking, and definitely not words befitting a Queen. Instead, she turned to Belle, who had been walking on her other said, and said, "Call the Glory to a halt."

Bracing herself, she awaited the dragon's arrival.

Firethroat was not in a good mood. Having to deliver the Queen's message to Beloved, who was responsible for the disaster now shaking Luster, had left a bad taste in her mouth. It would have been much simpler, and far more pleasant, to simply eat the monstrous woman. But she knew a hundred Hunter arrows would have pierced her chest before she could have gotten close enough to enact that delightful solution. So she had carried out the task as it had been given to her.

When she spotted the Gathered Glory, she banked slightly to the right. Knowing that most of the unicorns were still not comfortable in her presence, she chose to land about a hundred feet away from the group. It gratified her to see that they had come to a standstill. At least that was a proper show of respect.

The unicorns maintained their distance, but after a

few moments one approached. Firethroat recognized him as Moonheart, the Queen's brother.

"We are glad to see you safely returned, my lady," he said. "We have sent for Amalia. I will wait for her to join us to hear how your task went.

Firethroat heard something odd in his voice, and wondered what it indicated. Well, she suspected she would find out soon enough. She settled on her haunches to wait for the Queen.

"You two stay here," Amalia told Belle and Feng Yuan when they reached the edge of the Glory.

Feng Yuan began to protest. "But my Queen, I should — "

"That was an order," replied Amalia sharply. "And I expect it to be obeyed!" Turning to her brother, she said, "That goes for you as well, Moonheart."

Moonheart looked as if he wanted to protest, but the Queen's voice left no room for that. He simply nodded his head in acknowledgment. He understood the danger, and understood as well that should anything happen to his sister, he would be the one who would have to take up leadership of the Glory. They could not take the risk of losing both of them to the dragon's wrath should it erupt.

By herself, Amalia walked forward until she was close enough to speak to Firethroat, and also out of range of the others.

"Greetings, and welcome, Firethroat. I hope your

safe return indicates success in your mission."

"It does indeed," said Firethroat. "Beloved has accepted your challenge." She tipped her head sideways and studied the Queen for a moment, then said, "Clearly you are troubled. What is it that bothers you even though I come to report a success?"

The Queen drew a deep breath, then said, "I need to ask still more of you. Tonight we plan to attack Beloved in her camp. I hope that you will join us."

Firethroat stared at Amalia, momentarily at a loss for words. When she finally did manage to speak, her voice held a mix of anger and astonishment. "That is not the message that you asked me to deliver!" she roared.

"No, it is not."

"You lied to me!"

"Yes, I did."

"You did it knowing that I myself cannot lie."

"Precisely," said Amalia.

"You took advantage of me."

"I admit to that as well."

"You do know that I could roast you where you stand!"

The Queen flinched, but said only, "I took that into account, and decided the risk was worth it."

Firethroat stared at the unicorn for another long moment before emitting a deep, rumbling sound. The noise terrified Amalia, until she realized that the dragon was laughing — something she had never imagined possible.

"You're not angry, then?" she asked when the Firethroat's laughter had subsided.

"I was when you explained what you had done. And perhaps I should be now. But I am more impressed with the cleverness of it. Since there was no way that I could have delivered that false information to Beloved had I known it was a lie, it was, I suppose, your only option. You were shameless in doing it, but this is a matter of life and death. Luckily for you, since I spoke the truth as I understood it at the time, I feel no compulsion to go back and correct the misinformation I gave that wretched woman."

"That is indeed a great relief," said the Queen.

"But don't ever do it again!" said the dragon, and this time there was a ferocity in her voice that made the Queen tremble.

"I doubt I would have the courage to try it a second time," replied Amalia.

Firethroat made a harumphing sound, then said simply, "What can I do next to help, you conniving wench of a Queen?"

Amalia laughed, then told the dragon the rest of their plan.

18

TUNNELING

Luster: Delvharken

The next time the stone walls began to shift Rocky embarrassed himself by screaming. He could not help himself. But his terror was not on his own behalf; it was for his teacher.

The movement of the stone lasted only a few moments. When it was done he turned to M'Gama and cried, "Is he alive? Surely you can tell if Namza still lives!"

Some ten feet away, Rocky's teacher did indeed find himself, much to his own astonishment, still alive. Though the stonefall had sealed the narrow shaft through which he had been crawling, he had managed to reach the air pocket. Unfortunately, during the temblor the space had been compressed so that it was now barely bigger than his own tiny body. His relief at being alive was so great it took a moment for him to realize that his right foot was trapped.

Ignoring the pain, which was intense and growing worse, Namza stretched out his mind to contact the Geomancer.

M'Gama's eyes flew open. "He lives!"

Rocky gasped in relief.

"Be still," ordered the Geomancer. "Your teacher and I have work to do." Closing her eyes, she relaxed into herself, then entered the Stone once more. When she and Namza were in solid contact, she thought, *Shall we begin?*

I see no point in delay. And I am rather eager to leave this space if I can.

He did not mention the trapped foot.

Once more they linked their magics, straining to force the Stone to their will. But though they exercised all their power, nothing happened.

We need my student to join us, thought Namza at last.

Is he ready for this?

Not at all. In fact, it may well destroy him. But the three of us — not to mention the world itself — are already at the edge of destruction.

I will see what I can do, replied M'Gama.

Namza sighed and settled in to wait, which was not easy, given that tons of rock seemed ready to crush his finger-sized body.

"We need your help," M'Gama said to Rocky.

"Of course! I'll do anything!"

M'Gama made a sound of exasperation. "I wish people would think before they say such things. Oh, trust me," she added quickly, "you're not the only one. But I need you to understand that we are asking you to take part in a magic for which you are not ready. It may well be more than you can bear."

"What I cannot bear is to lose my teacher! What must I do?"

M'Gama sighed. The rate at which she was becoming connected to these delvers was alarming! To Rocky she said, "Take my hands and I will pull you into the magic. Your biggest task will be to let go — first let go of your body, and then let go of your fear, for both will block what we are trying to do. Mostly we need to draw on your energy. Have you practiced this at all with your teacher?"

"Only once, and it was . . . not a success."

"Well, it had better succeed now. Otherwise this will be our permanent resting place." To herself, she added, *At least, I think it will be our permanent resting place.* The truth was, she had no idea what would happen if Luster actually split apart . . .which was beginning to seem more and more likely.

Rocky reached forward and took her hands.

"Ready?" she asked.

"Ready."

She drew him into the magic.

Rocky felt as if his soul were being plucked from his body. This was different from when he had nearly fallen into the Stonesleep. Then he was, in a way, returning to where he belonged, or at least his body was. Now he felt as if part of him were going somewhere it did not belong at all. Panic seized him, and he began to fight the magic.

Stop struggling! ordered M'Gama. *You will do yourself no good and in fact will make things worse for all of us.*

Rocky wanted to take a deep breath to calm himself, but since he was no longer in his body that was not possible.

Do you trust your teacher? demanded M'Gama.

Yes. YES!

Then please, trust me as his partner in this magic. You will be with him soon, I promise.

That did the trick. Thinking of Namza, Rocky was able to hold himself together just long enough for M'Gama to finish the linking. Once secure in the presence of his teacher, he let go of his fear and began to observe.

His first thought was that it was beautiful to see what M'Gama and Namza were doing, which was weaving their very selves into the Stone. Soon he began to understand how it worked. After several minutes he relaxed and joined them.

At first they simply pulled parts of him along with them, but after a little while he was able to participate in the work.

Despite all this, he was shocked by the burst of pain he felt when they actually began to shift the stone. For a moment he nearly lost consciousness. The strain was incredible, but he held on, held on, held on. . . .

A terrible grinding sound began, the sound of stone reluctantly moving at their command, compacting itself, opening a way for them to pass.

Though the tunnel they created was only about ten feet long, the work took hours. Namza and M'Gama set things in motion, but it was Rocky's youthful strength that let them finish the job, though they pulled so much energy from him to do so that when it was over he was barely able to move.

After the Geomancer and the delver returned to their bodies, they crawled — dragged themselves, really — through the tunnel. Rocky went first, taking a moment to gather up Namza's robes before he began. He was about halfway along when something dropped onto his bald scalp. He barely stopped himself from brushing it away before he realized it must be Namza. "Teacher?" he asked softly.

"Yes, it's me," replied Namza, crawling past his student's ear and onto his shoulder. "I do not have the strength to return to my normal shape right now, so I must ask you to carry me."

"It will be my honor."

"Will you please keep moving?" snapped M'Gama from behind them. "I do not want to be in this tunnel when the next tremor hits!"

Rocky scurried forward. When he climbed down from the far side of their narrow tunnel, he emerged into a regular delver tunnel that was, amazingly, unbroken. He was delighted to see that the orange lines along its side were still glowing. M'Gama emerged shortly afterward. Accepting Namza's continued lizardhood — he was still perched on Rocky's shoulder— without comment, she said simply, "Which way to the surface?"

Rocky wept as they made their way out of Delvharken.

He wept not because the journey was hard, though it was. They had to negotiate great rifts in the floors of the tunnels. They came to massive stonefalls nearly impossible to pass. In several places they feared the ceiling was but moments from collapsing onto their heads.

No, it was the destruction — which was even worse now than when he had made his way underground not long before — that drew his tears. He wept, too, for the work itself, for the craft and the care that had gone into creating the tunnels and gateways, the smooth floors and the perfect angles of Delvharken. Those passageways were the work of generations of delvers, and it had taken but days for all that labor to be swept away. Most of all he wept because if stone itself was not solid and safe, then nothing was.

Namza was more resigned, but seemed to understand what Rocky was feeling, for he often muttered soothing words from his perch on his pupil's shoulder.

M'Gama did not speak much for the first part of the journey, but finally she stopped and turned to Rocky. When the delver stopped, too, she dropped to her knees so she could be face-to-face with lizard-Namza.

"When your student asked me to pull you back from the Stone he told me he believed you were the only one who could halt this destruction. Yet you claim you know no way of doing so. Were your student's words just a ruse to gain my help?"

Namza took a long time to answer, and M'Gama had to lean close to hear when he finally did speak. "I can do nothing to stop this myself. However, I do know of one who might accomplish it. Unfortunately, he has not been heard from in hundreds of years."

"Who is it?" asked Rocky eagerly.

"You have known of him as 'the Great One.'"

M'Gama snorted in disgust. "A delver myth is not going to help us now."

"He is not a myth," insisted Namza, though he did not seem offended. "There truly was . . . *is* . . . a Great One. His name was Elihu. He may seem to have disappeared, but I tell you truly he is still a part of Luster."

"What are you talking about?" asked M'Gama.

Before Namza could answer, they heard a roar behind them — not the sound of falling rock, but the cry of some great beast.

"What is that?" asked the Geomancer.

"Hard to say," replied Namza, his forked tongue flicking out with each word. "Any number of strange creatures haunt the deeper parts of Delvharken. It would make sense that they, too, are making their way to the surface. You and I might be able to battle such a beast, lady. Even so, I suspect it would be wiser to flee."

M'Gama glanced behind her and quickly agreed.

"This reminds me of the time I was fleeing the skwartz," panted Rocky, after they had run up a long, sloping tunnel and turned a tight corner.

"You attracted a *skwartz* and lived to tell of it?" asked Namza in astonishment.

"I had help. I was with a human girl, a gryphon, and an old dwarf named Grimwold."

"Student," said Namza, "it is clear you have a great deal to tell me when the time is right. Even so, for the moment I would suggest we talk less and move faster."

Another roar from behind, clearly closer now than the last time they had heard it, underlined his point.

They quickened their pace and soon came to a wide corridor, partially blocked by rubble. With a glad cry of "There's the way out!" Rocky turned to enter it.

"Not there!" said Namza urgently.

"But we want to go to the surface. This is the main exit."

"If we're planning to go to the Axis Mundi, I know

a better way. There's a transit point not far off. Follow my directions."

Soon they turned into a side tunnel that, after about a hundred feet, ended at a solid wall.

"What treachery is this?" demanded M'Gama.

"Any treachery lies in our sharing this with you," replied Rocky sharply. "This is a transit point. It is one of the great secrets of the delvers. Look more closely, Geomancer."

Barely visible in the dim light was the outline of an arch in the wall. Even harder to see were the odd symbols carved around it. Tracing them with his fingertip, Rocky began to chant.

Another bellow from the beast pursuing them overpowered his voice.

"Whatever you're doing, you'd better do it fast," cried M'Gama. "That thing is at the mouth of the tunnel!"

Fingers trembling, still chanting, Rocky finished tracing the symbols.

The space within the arch began to glow.

"Hurry!" cried the delver.

With Namza still on his shoulder, he stepped through the arch and disappeared.

M'Gama followed, crying out at the cascade of tingles that flowed over her skin. As soon as she was through, Rocky turned and, again, began tracing symbols. "The transit point would seal by itself in a little while," explained Rocky. "But we don't want to take a chance of that thing getting through before it does!"

"What just happened?" demanded M'Gama, shuddering with the aftereffects of passing through the transit point. "I felt the same tingling several times when I was carried into Delvharken. But I was blindfolded then, and could never tell what was going on."

"These spots are shortcuts," said Rocky, who had finished his chanting. "You step through them in one place and come out in another."

"How do they work?"

"That is deep magic," said Namza. "As is the fact that we are now quite close to the Axis Mundi."

As if to underscore where they now stood, the tunnel shook more violently than ever.

"The disruption is greatest here, closest to the tree," said M'Gama, her face grim. "We must get above ground as quickly as possible."

"The exit is not far," said Namza. "May I suggest that we run?"

It was just as well that they did, since as they were emerging from the tunnel it collapsed behind them with a thunderous roar. The explosive impact pushed them forward and surrounded them with another choking cloud of dust. Coughing and gasping for breath, they staggered onward.

It was dusk when they emerged, so though there was some light, it was not enough to hurt Rocky's eyes. They were in a forest, which made things even darker. However not far ahead they could see a lighter area, indicating that the forest thinned. Pointing toward it, M'Gama said, "That must be the edge of the meadow that surrounds the tree."

TUNNELING

As she began to stride forward Rocky said, "Wait, please. I need to call my cousins. They were expecting to meet me here should I manage to return from Delvharken. They may have news for us."

M'Gama turned back and watched as Rocky lowered himself to the ground. He set Namza's robes beside him, then crossed his hands over his chest. Having done this recently, it did not take him long to move into the trancelike state that let him make the call.

As Rocky sat, Namza limped down his student's arm, then over his abdomen. He made his way to the ground, then crawled a few feet away. M'Gama watched in fascination as he slowly returned to his delver form. When the transformation was finished, he fell backward, panting, his eyes closed in anguish.

Concerned, the Geomancer went to his side.

"I will be all right," he said. "I just need time to recover. Making such a change is . . . painful." He paused, then said, "Would you hand me my robes? And if you know any spells for stanching the flow of blood, you might apply one to my foot."

She glanced down and gasped at the sight of his torn and twisted toe.

"It was caught in the movement of rock while I was in the tunnel," he explained. "I managed to halt the bleeding then, but the transformation has opened it again."

M'Gama hesitated, then pulled one of the jeweled rings from the fingers of her left hand. Murmuring a low chant, she slipped the ring over Namza's big toe.

After a moment, the pulse of blood stopped.

"Keep that on for now," she said as she handed him his robes. "Not only will it help with the bleeding, it will help hold the pain at bay."

"Thank you," Namza said, managing to get to his feet. "I welcome the relief. The pain was making it hard to think."

As Rocky had predicted, it did not take long for the first of his cousins — again, it was Gratz, now known as Pebble — to sense the call.

Knowing the connection had been made, Rocky moved back to full wakefulness. He smiled to see his teacher in his true form again, then said proudly, "The rest of my cove will be here soon."

Indeed, ten minutes and two tremors later, a group of seven delvers came trotting into view.

19

CONVERGENCE

Luster: The Axis Mundi

It didn't make any difference what you had been told in advance, the first time you saw the Axis Mundi, you could not help but gasp in awe.

At least, that was Cara's reaction when she, Fallon, Medafil, and the Squijum reached the edge of the meadow that surrounded the great tree. Until that moment, the true height and width of the Axis Mundi had been hidden by the lesser trees through which she and her companions were walking. Seen suddenly in its full glory, the tree was breathtaking.

Except it was also heartbreaking, because at its base gaped a ragged opening that Cara realized must mark where Beloved had blasted her way into Luster. Even more appalling, it was clear that the wound she had created was growing, extending upward, splitting the massive trunk like a spreading infection.

Cara took a step forward, then cried out and pulled back in shock. The meadow was rippling, the ground rolling and lurching as if massive snakes, yards wide and hundreds of feet long, squirmed and twisted just beneath its surface.

The Squijum chattered in alarm and tightened his grip on Cara's mane. At the same time Medafil spread his wings, crying, "Gaaah! What in the froomp-dingled world is happening?"

"The roots of the tree are in pain," replied Fallon softly.

Cara turned away, sickened. In that turning, she spotted a cove of delvers standing not far away. They, too, had stopped at the edge of the meadow. Like her own group, they were staring at the ground with clear dismay. Their presence would have been yet one more reason for concern, if not for the fact that in their midst stood the Geomancer.

Cara blinked, startled. What was M'Gama doing with a group of delvers? She had always hated the creatures.

Of course, Cara admitted to herself, her own feelings about delvers had changed drastically, at least in regard to Rocky. So it was certainly possible M'Gama might have befriended some as well. Even so, Cara's first reaction was to fade back into the forest, hoping Fallon and Medafil would follow her lead. But an instant later — thanks to her improved eyesight — she realized one of the delvers was her own dear Rocky. At least, she thought it was Rocky. What had happened to his face? It was scored with a series of wavy marks that looked like dark tattoos.

Leaning toward Fallon, she murmured, "A cove of delvers stands to our right. Normally I would suggest we retreat, but one of them is a friend of mine, as is the tall woman in their midst."

"Then let us join them," said Fallon.

No sooner had the words passed his lips than Cara cursed herself for not thinking more quickly. Neither Rocky nor M'Gama would be able to recognize her now that she was a unicorn. So how was she going to explain to Fallon that she had just claimed them as friends?

Well, Lightfoot spoke passable delvish, she reminded herself. *So it's not as if Rocky hasn't spoken to a unicorn before. And Fallon won't understand what I say when I speak delvish. Maybe I can pull this off.*

Taking a deep breath, she called, "Rocky!"

Instantly she felt more a fool than ever. Her grandmother had always said truth was the simplest thing, and that was certainly true right now. What was not simple was that there was no way that, as a unicorn, she should have known her delver friend now went by the nickname she herself had given him. She braced for his questions, desperately hoping she could get her story straight.

The delvers turned toward the call and immediately began to chatter. Rocky said something — Cara couldn't hear what — and the others fell silent.

Apparently he was now their leader.

The two groups walked toward each other until they were about twenty feet apart. Staring at her curiously, Rocky said, "How is it, unicorn, that you know my nickname?"

Medafil, seeing that Cara was fumbling for an answer, asked softly, "What did he say?"

When she had translated for him the gryphon stepped forward and said, "I told her, of course, you silly delver!"

Cara shot him a grateful look, then translated his comment for Rocky.

The delver nodded. "It is good to see you again, Medafil. Though it has not been that long since we traveled together, the world is changing rapidly."

Cara translated, as she continued to do throughout the conversation.

"Too rapidly, sot-groggle it," agreed the gryphon.

"Who are your friends?" asked Rocky.

Gesturing with his wing, Medafil said, "The unicorn goes by the name of Silverhoof."

As she translated this, Cara admired the way the gryphon had shaped the sentence to make it both deceptive — and absolutely true.

"The Squijum you know, of course," continued Medafil. "The tall gentleman goes by the name of Fallon."

"And how is it, Silverhoof, that you speak delvish?" Rocky asked, addressing her directly.

"I . . . learned it from my friend, Prince Lightfoot."

This was a lie. The truth was that Firethroat had granted Cara "the gift of tongues," which let her speak all languages, as a reward for a great service the girl had rendered her.

"Ah," replied Rocky. "And I see that you have the Squijum on your back. As far as I know, he is the only one of his kind. He used to travel with a friend of mine called Cara. Seeing him without her makes me fear she has suffered some mishap."

Cara translated this for Medafil, partly as a way to give herself time to think. To her relief, he again answered for her, saying, "I saw Cara not long ago. She was fine at the time. As to the Squijum — well, you know as well as I that he's a flighty little creature. You're apt to find him anywhere."

The Squijum made a rude sound and pinched Cara's neck, but said nothing.

Rocky nodded.

Seeing that the delver had accepted his explanation, Medafil said, "In return, and remembering that you are an exile from Delvharken, I am wondering who travels with you and how it is that you are here at the Axis Mundi."

"These are my cousins," said Rocky, gesturing toward the cove. "Just as Cara gave me a nickname, I have done the same for them. They are now known as

Lizard, Waterfall, First, Hammer, Diamond, Pebble, and Wart."

Looking at the delvers, each of whom bowed as introduced, Cara could not help but think, *They're sort of like the Seven Dwarfs, except half naked and much stranger looking.*

Gesturing to his right, Rocky continued, "And this is Namza. He is my teacher and the wisest of all delvers. The tall human is someone you must certainly have heard of, if not actually met — M'Gama, the Geomancer."

M'Gama stepped forward. Speaking in the language of the unicorns, she said, "What brings us here is the troubling of the tree. I would ask the same of you, as well as wondering who the human is who travels with you."

"As Medafil said, his name is Fallon," replied Cara.

"Not his name. Where did he come from and why are you all here?"

Cara turned to Fallon to translate this, then stopped cold. From the corner of her eye she had caught something she would never have noticed if not for the extended field of vision that had come with her transformation — something that set her heart pounding with joy.

The clearing that surrounded the tree was no longer empty. Coming toward them from the far side, stumbling their way across the writhing roots, were two humans and a unicorn.

Fallon, who had followed her gaze, hailed them. The smaller of the humans, a brown-skinned boy she guessed must be the "Rajiv" that Fallon had spoken of, raced ahead of the others. "Sahib Fallon!" he cried. "Sahib Fallon! I feared I would never see you again!"

Fallon caught the boy up — he seemed absurdly small next to the towering man — and swung him into the air. "I feared the same, Rajiv! I am glad the world has brought us together once more." He set the boy down beside him and rested one huge hand on the boy's jet-black hair as they awaited the arrival of the others.

The reunion of Rajiv and Fallon gave Cara time to still her beating heart, which her chest could barely contain, for the approaching unicorn was none other than her beloved Lightfoot. She longed to act just as Rajiv had with Fallon and to run to him! And she might have done just that, if not for the fact that the woman . . . the slender, graceful woman with the long red hair . . . was her mother.

Even without the improved vision that had come with the unicorn transformation, Cara would have recognized her; with that vision she could clearly discern, despite the distance between them, the features of a face that — other than a brief time in an enchanted dream — she had seen only in photographs for the last nine years. It was all she could do to stifle a sob of joy, and also hold in her impulse to race forward. In fact, she started to do just that before she caught herself, torn between longing and fear. What was she to say? How was she to explain to her mother that she, her long-lost daughter, was now a unicorn?

Then another question seized her, this one far more frightening: Fallon had said her parents were together when he left them. *So where was her father?*

Lightfoot uttered a cry of greeting, a sound that made Cara's heart leap with responding joy, even though it was Fallon the Prince called out to, not her. But an instant later the same concern she had had regarding her mother overwhelmed her again. What would *Lightfoot* think of what she had done?

To her surprise, she realized she was hoping he would welcome the change, even be delighted by it.

The trio's approach was made slower by the fact that after a few steps they backed away from the rippling meadow, choosing to walk around its perimeter instead. When they were finally within speaking distance, Fallon said, "Greetings, Prince. And greetings, Mrs. Hunter. I am extremely pleased to see you, but concerned that your husband is not with you."

"We are hoping he will be here soon," said Martha. Quickly she explained what had happened since they had last seen each other.

Cara's heart sank as she listened, and it was all she could do to keep from wailing in despair. Had she found her mother only to lose her father? The thought that he might have traveled all the way into Delvharken in search of her not only terrified her, it filled her with a wrenching guilt. How would they ever get him back? What if that cavernous world collapsed on him while he was down there looking for her?

Her bleak thoughts were interrupted by M'Gama stepping forward again. At her side was the old delver Rocky had introduced as "Namza."

Cara, who had grown used to the strange looks of the creatures during her time with Rocky — indeed, had come to accept it as just part of who they were — was momentarily startled by the way her mother recoiled at the sight of the aged delver.

Namza was staring at Fallon intently. Finally he said, "I have met someone like you before, tall one. Who are you, and what brings you to this world?"

Cara began to translate this from delvish, but Fallon startled her by saying, "Never mind, Silverhoof. I can understand him." Turning to the delver, his eyes more intense than Cara had ever seen them, he said, "Who was it that you met, venerable one?"

Though Fallon did not speak in delvish, it was clear the old delver understood him. She wondered if the big man had some version of the gift of tongues. If so, had he understood all her conversations with Rocky?

"Her name was Allura," said Namza.

Fallon closed his eyes and heaved a great sigh. "And what was the story she told?"

"You are of the same race as she, are you not?"

"Race is not the word I would use. However, you are correct that we are different from humans. We can discuss that later — assuming there is a later. For now, the story?"

"Let us move away from the meadow," replied Namza. "I mislike looking on that heaving ground."

This met with quick agreement from everyone, so the entire group — counting the Squijum there were now sixteen of them — moved into the forest until they found a space large enough to hold them. To Cara's mingled delight and concern, her mother — who she noticed had been looking at her oddly, as if she sensed something strange about her but could not figure out exactly what it was — took a place right next to her. Cara found herself leaning toward her, drinking in her scent and the sound of her every breath.

Namza began to speak again. Fallon served as translator, so that Martha, Rajiv, and Medafil could understand the tale the old delver unfolded.

"It is a sad story," he began, "and I know it only because this woman, Allura, appeared to me on the night of my teacher's death. She had come to honor him, which moved me. After he returned to the Stone, she told me this story. She said she thought the day would come when I would need to know."

He looked at Fallon as he said this, but the big man only nodded.

Seemingly satisfied with this, Namza continued. "As you may know, someone named Elihu officiated at the unicorns' great Purification Ceremony, the one that led to the birth of the Whisperer and ultimately the creation of the delvers."

"I've been told of that ceremony," said Fallon, unhappiness thick in his voice. "But try as I might,

I cannot understand why he would have done such a thing."

"According to Allura, he wanted perfect creatures for the perfect world he was trying to create."

"That is correct, old one," said a new voice. "You remember the story well."

All eyes turned in the direction from which the words had come.

Standing a few feet from their gathering place was a tall, brown-skinned, golden-haired woman.

With a squeal of joy the Squijum leaped from Cara's shoulder and went running to the woman. She held out her hand and the Squijum leaped to take it. Then he scrambled up her arm and onto her shoulder. The little creature looked as happy as Cara had ever seen him.

"Well," said Fallon, "this is a welcome surprise. It's good to see you again, my dear sister."

20

ENTER THE PLAYERS

Luster: Beloved's Encampment

Darkness was drawing on and the watch fires had been set in Beloved's camp when a quartet of brightly decorated wagons came rattling into the meadow southwest of the Axis Mundi. Three of the wagons were drawn by teams of four men. The fourth was pulled by an eccentric-looking man in a patchwork coat. He handled the wagon by himself, so easily it was as if it were weightless.

The wagons had not come far past the meadow's edge when a group of twenty Hunters, led by the man named Kenneth, gathered in front of them. "Who are you?" he demanded. "And what do you want here?"

ENTER THE PLAYERS

"Who are we?" cried the short, roundish man who rode atop the first wagon. "Why we are the famous Strolling Players of Luster!" He sprang to the ground with astonishing agility. "I, personally, am Armando de la Quintano, leader of the Players. We travel from north to south, east to west, putting on shows for the humans who live here. Word of a new group of humans reached us not long ago, so naturally we came as fast as we could. What more could Players want than a fresh audience?"

"Well, you can just turn around and travel back on out of here," snarled Kenneth. "We don't want any of your foolishness."

"You do not want entertainment?" asked Armando. He sounded astonished. "There is little in daily life to lift the heart, and not enough for men to see or to laugh at." With a leer he added, "We, on the other hand, travel with beautiful women. Their costumes, what there is of them, are . . . lovely!"

The men behind Kenneth began to grumble. "Let's have a show!" cried one of them.

"A good way to relax before tomorrow's battle!" called another.

"A battle?" cried Armando. "Good gracious! Well, it is a fact known 'round the world that men of war grow bored without some entertainment. Restless men are not good for discipline."

"Leave this place now," growled Kenneth.

"Oh, don't be such a prig, Ken!" cried a Hunter. "Let's have the show!"

"A show!" cried several others. "We want a show!"

Before Kenneth could say anything in response, Armando called, "Li Yun, come out and greet our audience!"

Instantly an exquisitely beautiful Asian woman, dressed in a gauzy costume that covered little more than necessary, sprang from the first cart. After a brief but highly athletic dance, she disappeared back into the cart.

The men cheered wildly and called for more.

Kenneth sighed. Though Beloved had retreated to her pavilion for the night, there were still hours to go before the men would sleep. And there was restlessness all across the camp. Maybe a show would be a good idea. "Oh, all right," he said. "Let's have your show, player."

"I am so pleased!" cried Armando. "We love to perform!"

Within a half hour, the main body of the Hunters was gathered on a slope on the southern side of the camp. The four wagons formed a half circle on the lower ground, and the Players had set out enough torches to provide plenty of light. Armando blew a battered horn, and the show began.

About a hundred yards away were two more players. They were dressed all in black, their usual costume for performing. But instead of entering with the wagons, they had wriggled across the meadow from the far side, pausing only when they were close enough to the encampment to observe what was happening. Now they lay belly down in the grass, watching intently.

"Looks like they're in place, Bert," said one of them.

"Coo, Alfie, I 'ope this works. I don't want to lie here henny longer than I 'ave to. I keep fearing the world's goin' to hopen under me belly and drop me down to lor' knows where!"

"I know what you mean, Bert. But standin', sittin', or lyin' here, there, or anywhere don't seem to make no difference. Everyplace is dangerous right now!"

First to perform was a trio of acrobats. Despite their best efforts, the Hunters responded with scant applause. Next Armando brought out Li Yun and two other women, who performed a dance that was greeted much more enthusiastically.

After they were finished, an older man, gloomy-looking in the extreme, came out and launched into a story that soon had the Hunters laughing so hard tears were streaming down their faces. He looked startled at provoking such amusement, which only doubled the merriment.

When he had finished, five female acrobats did a tumbling set that left the Hunters gasping with astonishment.

Then the back door of the fourth cart opened and out stepped the eccentric-looking man who had hauled it into the clearing to begin with. His bald head shone in the flickering light of the torches. He wore an absurdly colorful patchwork coat. The front of it was crisscrossed by numerous gold chains, each of which disappeared into one of the coat's equally numerous pockets.

Behind him, led by a much thicker chain, came the most ridiculous-looking creature anyone in the audience had ever seen. About half the man's height, it looked like a cross between a rooster and a dragon. A white cloth had been bound around its head, covering the eyes. That head itself was similar to a rooster's, though much larger and fiercer, especially around the beak. Below the head a long, scaly neck stretched down to a winged body that was also scaled, but had a thick fringe of feathers. Two stocky legs ended in clawed feet that were absurdly large for a creature of that size. Arcing up behind the creature was its tail. Though scaly and whiplike, it ended in a luxuriant plume of iridescent feathers.

The Hunters began to laugh, which was only natural. The creature was ridiculous, and none of them had any idea what a cockatrice was actually capable of. . . .

Across the meadow Alfie nudged Bert. "That beast is our cue!" he hissed. "Let's go!"

Bolting to their feet, the two men sprinted in opposite directions, eager to deliver their message to the waiting dragons.

ENTER THE PLAYERS

* * *

Unaware of what was happening on the hillside, Beloved was in her pavilion, casually tormenting Ian. It had become a way for her to relax between the times when she was hearing reports or issuing new orders. The torments were not physical. That was too easy and did not suit her purposes. She found it far more amusing to taunt him with his failure.

Her sorry descendant was sitting up now, as he was bound to the center pole of the tent. Because the delver paste that had sealed his lips had worn off, she now had him gagged. She had no interest in hearing whining excuses or petulant accusations. It was sufficient to watch his eyes, which sometimes blazed with hate, other times went dark with despair and defeat.

It was a distraction — and she always needed distraction from her pain, which rose and fell in waves, but was never totally absent.

The pavilion itself was a bit of an indulgence, with its plethora of cushions, all beautifully embroidered, most with designs and images based on the hunting of unicorns. She delighted to remember how many kings and nobles had heeded her urgings to kill the beasts all those centuries ago, back when the foul creatures still roamed the hills and forests of Earth, before that fool Bellenmore provided them with an escape route.

"Did you really think you could abandon me and not pay the price, Ian?" she purred now.

She was peeling an apple. Her long, slender fingers moved with languid grace. But the sense of relaxation was belied by her silver hair, which shifted and curled restlessly about her shoulders.

Ian, being gagged, made no answer.

"A pity you couldn't manage to capture that daughter of yours for me," she continued. "Things might have turned out differently if you had." The silver blade flashed as the bloodred peel of the apple descended from the fruit in a single, shining coil. "I meant her no harm," she went on softly. "It's just that she was potentially a . . . problem. I didn't realize that at first, of course. Ridiculous to think that someone so important to me should be hidden away so thoroughly."

The crimson peel dropped to the rug at her feet.

"Really, I was disinclined to put much stock in the prophecy about a child in whom the bloodlines of Hunter and unicorn merged. It was just too absurd. And it took time for my . . . sources . . . to find out the truth about her. She's disappeared now, did you know that? It's quite sad really. I might have thought she was simply in hiding. But I've had a hundred men out searching for her with the help of tracking packets seeded with my own blood. Blood calls to blood, as you know. Anyway, they nearly had her a few days ago. Then she just . . . vanished. It seemed mysterious at first, but the answer was obvious enough: She's *dead,* poor thing."

Neither the gag nor Ian's determination to hold

himself aloof could stifle the groan that rose from his inner depths.

"The truly tragic part is, she was probably killed by one of those monsters she so foolishly thought worthy of protection. A pity, really. If we had managed to capture her earlier, we might have saved her."

She raised the apple and took a bite, her perfect teeth tearing at the fruit's white flesh.

Ian turned his head.

"Look at me!" snapped Beloved. When he did not obey, she stood, walked to him, grabbed his chin. With a grip that was remarkably powerful, she forced his head around so he was facing her once again. "A tear? Oh, dear me, Ian. I'm ashamed. I thought we had taught you to be stronger than that."

She started to say something else, but just then all hell broke loose.

21

THE PIECES OF THE PUZZLE

Luster: Near the Axis Mundi

Allura favored Fallon with a gentle smile. "I'm here for exactly the same reason you are, brother. I came because of Elihu." She turned to Namza. "I am sorry I could not get here sooner, venerable one. There is great risk for me in the journey from the Higher Realm, which is not done quickly. Yet even in my home, I felt it when the tree was disturbed. I have been trying to return here ever since that moment."

"It is a joy to see you again, lady," said Namza, bowing deeply.

Allura spread her hands in acknowledgment, then

turned back to Fallon. "It has been a long time, brother."

"Millennia," he replied. "And this was the last place I expected to find you, sister."

She shook her head. "Surely you must have known I would be doing whatever I could to keep track of Elihu. Not having been banished as you two were, I had more freedom — though I did suffer some suspicion simply because I was so close to both of you. Even so, I journeyed here as often as I could manage to escape the notice of the Higher Powers."

"Tell me what you know of Elihu's fate," said Fallon, his voice almost pleading.

Allura sighed. "It is not a happy tale. Nor is the fact that the punishment he suffered after you last saw him —"

"A new punishment?" cried Fallon.

She nodded grimly. "A new punishment, for a new transgression. You know how his passion for whatever he was trying to create could be endearing, compelling, and infuriating all at the same time. After the two of you were exiled, it grew beyond that. I think, perhaps, he went a little mad. His passion seemed to take him over and blind pride seized him, driving him to urge the unicorns to an ill-considered 'Purification Ceremony.'"

"Yes," said Fallon with a groan. "I know about that."

"But do you also know that in urging your unicorns to that act of pride he again offended the Higher

Powers? They were already angry with him for creating Luster, of course, as it was something far beyond his rank and station. Having one mark against him for that previous act of rebellion, his punishment this time was swifter . . . and far more devastating."

She paused as the ground shifted beneath them. When it began to settle, Fallon asked apprehensively, "What was this punishment, Allura?"

Looking directly at him, she replied, "The Powers transformed your *alahim* into a bestial creature that came to be known as the Dimblethum. Then they relegated him to Earth."

Fallon moaned. Cara let out a cry of astonishment. Lightfoot shook his head in disbelief.

Allura swallowed hard, as if trying to control her emotions, then continued her story. "Confused and unhappy, but not knowing *why* he was unhappy, Elihu — now trapped in this coarse, lumbering form — made his way across Earth to the place where it connects with the Axis Mundi of Luster. It is not a spot most men can reach or even see. But despite his transformation, as its creator he still maintained a connection to this world. Once at the Axis Mundi, he was able to travel the tree back here, to the place he now considered his true home.

"I kept watch on him when I was able and did small things to try to protect him. It was not easy, for Luster is a forbidden place and every trip I made here was dangerous for me." As she said this she stroked the Squijum, who was nestled behind the curtain of her golden hair. "I let my little companion here travel with me, until he disappeared on one of my trips."

"Hotcha good Squijum got losted," said a small voice from behind her hair.

"Yes," she said fondly, "you got losted and nearly broke my heart, you wicked creature." Looking up at the others, she said, "Happily, I see he has made friends on his own."

"You always were good at the small creatures, Allura," said Fallon wistfully.

His sister smiled at him, then continued her story. "The years — the centuries — that followed were hard for Elihu. Once so elegant and graceful, so quick of eye, deft of hand, and sharp of wit, he now lived under a cloud, his body coarse and shambling, his keen mind dulled and foggy. He was lost and miserable, but did not know *why* he was lost and miserable. And he was intensely lonely, here in the world that he had created. At the same time, he was also intensely protective of it. When the unicorns finally did begin to arrive, he could not remember that the main reason he had urged them to undertake that disastrous Purification Ceremony was to make them good enough for his new world. He thought of them now as invaders and resented their presence."

Baffled by this, Cara intruded, asking, "But why were the unicorns coming here at all if Elihu no longer remembered these things?"

"He had informed an old magician named Bellenmore of his plans. Even though Elihu had seemingly vanished, when Beloved's Hunt of the unicorns grew ever more dangerous, Bellenmore and his apprentice, Aaron, followed through on the idea.

"As you know, Elihu's spirit was a restless one. Still inflamed with a desperate desire to create, even in his new brutish form he was always trying to make things. Yet he was continually thwarted by his clumsy paws and clouded brain. This was the true, and I think truly cruel, punishment of the Higher Powers. To punish his pride they did not merely cast him into this monstrous form, they blocked his deepest and most powerful urge."

She spread her hands, to indicate that she had finished her story. Cara stared at her for a long time before she finally said, "That was fascinating, but there must be some mistake. I've met Elihu!"

Allura looked at her in puzzlement.

"And I've seen the Dimblethum since then, too," she continued.

Even as the words passed her lips, Cara felt a sharp twist in her heart as she realized she was going to have to tell her story now — a realization confirmed when M'Gama said, "Tell us about this, Silverhoof."

The Geomancer's voice, always powerful, now held an air of command.

Cara glanced to her left. Her mother stood beside her, watching her with an expression she could not interpret, but that seemed to carry both fear and expectation. Lightfoot was on the other side of her mother, and Rajiv stood on the Prince's far side. Both had their hands on his shoulders, which Cara took to mean they could communicate with him mind-to-mind. Well, at least that would make things easier. She could tell the story in delvish and let Lightfoot provide the translation for the only two who could not understand that language.

"It happened three days ago. I was on the slopes of Dark Mountain with the dragon Graumag. We were heading for Autumngrove and had stopped to rest."

This was not the important information, but she had to build herself up to telling the full story.

"We had had a close encounter with some Hunters. We managed to elude them and were trying to decide what to do next, when Elihu entered the place where we were resting. He looked a great deal like you, Fallon, but he wore an animal's skin." She hesitated, afraid to speak the next words, but knowing she had to. "Without warning, he snatched me up and carried me away."

Fallon looked at her in puzzlement. "Elihu is powerfully built, Silverhoof, but I don't understand how he could pick up a unicorn and run off with her."

Cara drew a deep breath, then said it: "I was not a unicorn at the time."

Now all eyes were riveted on her. Cara could tell — by her mother's gasp and the way her hand flew to her mouth — the exact moment this information passed from Lightfoot to her.

Speaking quickly before she lost her courage, Cara continued her story. "He snatched me up to protect me, because he had heard Hunters approaching. He was swift and strong, and he carried me to a cave. And there . . . there . . ."

"What happened?" demanded her mother.

Cara turned toward Martha Hunter and spoke her next words in English. "He offered to turn me into a unicorn so I could escape the Hunters, who were searching for me in my true form."

Tears rolled down Martha Hunter's face as she whispered, "And what was that true form?"

Cara's response rose on a half-choked sob. "My true form? It was the human shape I was born in." She swallowed hard. "I was called Cara, Cara Diana —"

Before she could finish, her mother flung herself forward. Wrapping her arms around Cara's neck she cried, "I knew it! I *knew* it was you the moment I saw you! I don't know how. It made no sense, it was mad, insane. But my heart knew the truth. I knew you were my daughter!"

She buried her face against Cara's silky mane and sobbed. As did Cara, who longed for arms so that she could hold her mother, as her mother held her. "It's all right, Mom," she whispered, not knowing what else to say.

She felt Lightfoot press against her other side. "Thank the Bright Powers you're safe," he thought. "I've been so worried about you!"

She wished they could stay like this forever.

But the writhing world would not allow that.

It was Fallon who finally came to them. Putting an arm around Martha's shoulders, he murmured, "I know this is overwhelming for you, Mrs. Hunter. But the world is dying, and it will not wait for us to work out the matters closest to our hearts." Glancing at Allura, he added, "Believe me, I say this with painfully unfinished matters of my own. But we must press on in search of the truth."

Martha nodded and managed to calm herself. But she did not let go of Cara's neck.

At that moment, Rocky stepped forward. Next to him stood another delver. Rocky nudged him, then nudged him again.

"My name is Lizard," said the new delver. "I do not like to bring more bad news, but I feel I should tell you that Ian Hunter is a prisoner of Beloved."

"How do you know this?" cried Cara, her joy at being reunited with her mother pierced by new terror.

"We were spying on her camp, which is in a meadow southwest of the great tree, not too far from here. We saw some delvers carry him in, bound and gagged. They took him to Beloved's tent, and later two Hunters carried him inside."

Lizard stepped back, as if embarrassed to have been speaking in front of so many people.

"We have to go get him!" cried Martha.

"First we must finish untangling this puzzle," said

Fallon. "If the world fails, Ian will be lost, anyway. If we can figure out a way to save Luster, then we can work to save him as well."

Cara trembled with frustration, but knew that Fallon was right.

It was Allura who spoke next. "I do not understand how Elihu can once more be in his true form. How could he have escaped the judgment of the Higher Powers?"

At that, Lightfoot stepped into the conversation. "I fear I know the answer."

All eyes turned toward the unicorn.

"Yes?" asked Allura.

Cara could hear both eagerness and dread in her voice.

"I saw the Dimblethum at the Axis Mundi the night Beloved forced her way into Luster. He was placing the wire sphere that M'Gama called an anchor onto a pillar of stone that was clearly made by delvers. I could not understand, then, why he would have done such a thing. Now I believe . . ."

His voice trailed off, unable to speak the terrible thing he suspected of the tortured creature who had been his friend.

After a long silence, Fallon said it for him: "You believe he betrayed Luster in return for being restored to his true shape."

"That is my fear," said Lightfoot mournfully.

"But who could have done that for him, who offered it to him?" asked Allura.

THE PIECES OF THE PUZZLE

"The Whisperer, of course," said Fallon grimly.

A cry escaped Martha's lips.

Fallon turned to her. "What is it, Mrs. Hunter?"

"I almost did something as bad," she murmured. "Indeed, I might have, had the chance arisen before we met you here. This Whisperer . . . he came to me last night and promised . . . promised —"

She broke off, unable to continue right away. Silence lay across the listeners as Martha fought past her shame. Finally she said softly, "He promised he would bring me to my daughter if I would help him capture my mother." Her face blazing with self-reproach, she added, "All I can say is, do not blame this Elihu of yours too much. The Whisperer is a demon of persuasion."

"But if the Dimblethum became Elihu again, where has he gone?" asked Namza.

"Alas, the answer to that is easy," replied Allura. "Well, not where he is. But I fear I can explain the why of his disappearance." Turning to Cara, she said, "There is a thing called Transformational Magic."

"I know. I learned about it from the dragon Graumag."

"That magic would be what the Whisperer used to return Elihu to his true form," explained Fallon, his face grim. "And that same magic, stored in his body after his return to his true shape, would be what Elihu used to transform you into a unicorn." He shook his head, golden hair flowing over his broad shoulders. "After all those years of suffering, he sacrificed what he had gained to save you."

"But why would he do that when Luster itself is at risk?" she cried, feeling yet another pang of guilt.

"I suspect he did not understand the full danger," said Fallon. "After returning to his true form, he must have been confused. He had spent several centuries as the Dimblethum. There is no telling what he could remember and what was lost to him."

"He was very fond of you, Cara," put in Lightfoot. "He would have been eager to protect you any way he could."

"I am sure he was wracked with guilt for what he had done," added Allura. "He would have been looking for a way to expiate his crime, a crime committed against the very thing he loved most, the world he had created."

"So if only Elihu can heal the tree, and Elihu is now the Dimblethum again, does that mean there is no hope for Luster?" asked Lightfoot.

As if to reinforce his question, another tremor shook the world.

"There is hope," replied Fallon, his face set and dark.

"There is always hope," agreed Allura. "But in this case it is faint and comes with a heavy price attached."

"And now," said Fallon, "if you will excuse me, I have a job to do."

"Where are you going?" asked Cara.

Face grim, voice low, he replied, "I must tend to this Whisperer."

With no more words than that, he loped away from them, disappearing into the forest.

Rocky nodded to his cove. Lizard nodded back. Without a sound, the cove turned and trotted after Fallon.

The remaining group was silent for a moment, a silence broken when Martha exclaimed, "Where is Rajiv?"

22

THE BLOODY FIELD

Luster: Beloved's Encampment

While the Hunters were absorbed by Armando's show, in the forest beyond the meadow the Gathered Glory waited tensely for the sign that the time was right to attack. Firethroat and Graumag were positioned at opposite ends of the glory's ranks. All it took was word from Bert and Alfie and suddenly two columns of flame shot straight into the air.

This was the signal the unicorns had been waiting for. With Belle and Moonheart at their front, the Gathered Glory began its first and only charge as an army. Racing out of the woods and across the meadow, they moved in silence at first. But when they reached the edge of Beloved's camp they trumpeted their fury at the invasion of their home.

With them came the Princess Arianna of the centaurs, her bowstring singing as she dispatched arrow after arrow into the ranks of the Hunters. Surging in on the left flank were Hiram Smith and the men of Sweetwater.

At the first sound, the Hunters sprang to their feet. Cursing and shouting, they drew swords, nocked arrows, raised spears. The ones in front of the audience turned their fury on the Players. As they did, Thomas whipped the blindfold off the ridiculous creature he had been displaying.

The effect was immediate and horrifying: The first three men that rushed forward turned instantly to stone.

"Don't look at it!" screamed one of the Hunters. *"Don't look at it!"*

But it's hard to battle something you can't see, and at least two Hunters, more brave than wise, tried to sink arrows into the cockatrice's heart. The drawing of their bows was the last movement they ever made. Their hands froze on the bowstrings, eternally holding shafts they would never let fly.

As the other Hunters turned away or covered their eyes, the Players launched their own well-planned attack. They flung themselves amongst the enemy, their lithe bodies twisting and turning as they struck out with fists and feet or slammed against the Hunters' backs, causing them to curse and stumble.

Two more men, foolish enough to turn back, fell victim to the gaze of the cockatrice.

Armando himself was working at ground level, rolling among the men, tripping as many as he could. They bellowed and thrust at him with sword or spear, but he was astonishingly fast for his girth. Still, he did not escape wounding, and blood flowed from several places on his body.

Tiny Li Yun leaped atop the back of another Hunter and covered his eyes with her hands. He turned, disoriented. At once she removed her hands, hiding her own face against his neck as she did.

It took her a moment to pull her legs free of his arms once he had turned to stone.

The cockatrice's toll was mounting, but the creature was clearly growing tired. Thomas saw that it could only manage one or two more petrifications before it collapsed in exhaustion.

Another Hunter had grabbed a torch and was trying to set fire to the players' carts. Jacques, launching into a series of handsprings, struck him in the back. The man fell, dropping the torch. Jacques quickly rolled him over it before it could set fire to the autumnal grass.

"Jacques!" called Thomas. "Give me a hand."

Turning, Jacques saw that the cockatrice was staggering and Thomas was tying the blindfold about its eyes once more. He hurried to join his friend. Quickly, the two men finished binding the beast, then hustled it into the cart.

"Shall we?" asked Thomas as they emerged once more.

"Yes, I think we should," said Jacques. He sprang forward and leaped into the fray even as the Tinker began pulling watches from his pockets. "Ah, this one will do," said Thomas. He raced up behind a Hunter who was grappling with one of the Players, opened the watch, and clamped it to the Hunter's ear. Instantly the man shrieked with pain and fell to the ground, clawing at the watch, which clung maddeningly to the side of his head.

The Player who Thomas had rescued looked at him with wide eyes. The Tinker shrugged and said, "I had forgotten how nasty that one is."

Despite these victories, the Players were not without their losses. Already three of them lay bleeding on the ground, one beyond all hope of recovery.

The fighting on the far side of the field was even more intense. The first wave of unicorns and Hunters had met, and the unicorns had trampled a number of the men under their feet. Yet these victories came with a cost, because even when he is down a man can thrust up with sword or spear. Now a flow of blood, both human and unicorn, was drenching that part of the field.

The battle raged on, made infinitely more difficult for both sides by the fact that they fought not on level ground, or even on solid ground, but on the surface of a world that was bucking and heaving in its death throes. Ever and again, a spear throw or sword thrust would go astray as the world lurched and a Hunter's legs buckled beneath him. Ever and again, a unicorn would rear, only to have the ground twist beneath its feet and send it crashing to its side.

Moonheart fought furiously, silver hooves flashing and flailing in the light.

Belle seemed to be everywhere at once, striking at Hunters while encouraging the unicorns. "Fight harder!" she cried over and over again. "Strike harder!"

She noted with approval that gentle Cloudmane was pressing forward, despite some terrible wounds, pummeling with front hooves, kicking with rear, an enraged fighting machine so ferocious that men were falling back in awe.

Even so, Belle knew in her heart that her people were not true warriors. Too many others held back their hoofblows, or struck askance, because their gentle hearts quailed at the thought of killing instead of healing.

"You fight for your lives and for the lives of your brothers and sisters, your mothers and fathers!" trumpeted Belle. "Fight, unicorns! Fight without pity! Fight without mercy! Fight, or we all die this night!

THE BLOODY FIELD

The dragons remained at the edge of the battle. The combat was so close that to shoot flame would wound as many friends as it would burn enemies.

In frustration, Firethroat finally plucked two of the men from the edge of the battle and simply ate them. Graumag, on the other hand, decided that this might be a good time to set the tents ablaze.

A moment later, Firethroat soared into the air. Turning, she flew *away* from the battle.

"Where is she going?" cried Feng Yuan, when she saw Firethroat veer away.

Along with the Queen and Alma Leonetti, the girl had been watching the battle from the edge of the forest.

"I do not know," Amalia Flickerfoot thought to the girl. "I cannot believe she is abandoning us. And she does not have a coward's heart. She must have her reason."

"I hope it is a good one," muttered Feng Yuan.

"Look!" cried Alma Leonetti, who was standing on the other side of the Queen, her hand also on the monarch's shoulder. "The tide is turning!"

Indeed, some of the Hunters were now turning and fleeing in the direction of the Axis Mundi. Yet despite the lift of hope this gave the Queen, her heart was sickened to see how many unicorns had already fallen in defense of their world.

Steel yourself against regret! Amalia commanded herself. *Even with all the blood, all the death, it will be worth it if the Hunt is ended forever.*

But then, just as it looked as if the enemy might indeed be ready to flee or surrender, a bloodcurdling ululation rose from the west side of the field. At first Amalia couldn't see the source of this cry, but a moment later she groaned in despair.

An army of delvers had come racing into the battle.

23

RAJIV STEPS IN

Luster: Beloved's Encampment

Rajiv had been horrified to learn that his friend the sahib was being held prisoner not far from where they stood. But as the intensity of the revelations that followed absorbed the rest of the group, it had been easy enough to slip away and disappear into the depths of the forest. Let the others fuss about the past. His job was to rescue his friend!

Because his sense of direction was good, and because he had known where they were coming from when they returned to the great tree, it did not take him long to figure out which way was southwest. However, he quickly discovered three great difficulties in actually moving through the forest. The first was the darkness that had fallen; oh, there was a half-moon, but its light hardly penetrated the deep woods. The second was the gaps that had opened in the ground; avoiding those slowed him considerably. The third was the number of trees that had been toppled as a result of the quakes. Some were huge and created massive barriers, their trunks as high as walls. Still, his clever fingers and nimble feet allowed him to scale the monsters. And when he came to the trunk of a fallen giant that actually created a bridge across a gap he might otherwise have been unable to cross, he blessed the tree for its sacrifice as he clambered onto its trunk.

Though it was wide enough that he could easily have walked along its surface, he chose, instead, to crawl, fearing that another tremor might cause the enormous thing to roll. It was well that he made this choice, for when he was only halfway across, the world did indeed shake again. The boy sank his fingers into the wide gaps in the tree's bark and clung to it as tightly as a chigger burrowing into flesh. Then the tree made quarter roll, leaving Rajiv gazing down into a yawning darkness for which he could see no bottom.

His position was terrifying, but not as terrifying as the thought that he might fail the sahib. He could not let that happen! He took stock of the situation: He was clinging to the trunk in a horizontal position. What was now the upper part of his "bridge" was a good twelve feet above him. He could not make it across from this position, so he needed to get back on top ... up to the new top. Tightening his knees against the trunk, he reached up with his left hand and grasped another of the bark's deep indentations. He wedged his fingers into the gap, relieved to find that he could get a solid hold. But when he tried to use his foot to bring his body level with his hands, he found that he could not get a decent grip with his boots on. He fervently wished that he was barefoot — a condition which he had been in for much of his life — for his nimble feet were much more flexible than the boots. But there was no way to rid himself of the clumsy things. Any attempt to kick them off would almost certainly dislodge him from his position. He tried again to gain a foothold, failed, then gasped in terror as his feet failed him altogether and he found himself clinging to the trunk with only his hands, his body dangling above the dark abyss.

He clenched his teeth, and in his mind vowed, *I will not fail you, Sahib Hunter.* Then he let go of the trunk with his right hand and reached upward.

To his relief, he quickly found purchase on another fold in the bark. With his feet dangling uselessly beneath him, acutely aware of the yawning emptiness eager to consume him, he continued to pull himself up. A sudden tremor shook his left hand loose. For a terrifying moment he hung from a single hand above the hungry gap below. With a strength aided by terror he lunged upward and regained his grip. Handhold by handhold, he made it to the top, where he sprawled across the comforting width of the tree, panting with relief.

But he had no time to relax. As soon as he had caught his breath, he started again, though this time not on his belly. Trusting to the world to give him a moment of grace, he scampered forward and made it safely to the far side of the trunk. With a huge sigh of relief he scrambled to the ground.

Given the ongoing tremors, the ground was hardly safe. Even so, it was more comforting and solid than the fallen tree trunk had been.

Rajiv had not traveled more than another ten minutes when he heard the clamor of a great battle. The unexpected sound confused him, but did seem to make it clear he was heading in the right direction.

When he emerged from the woods he saw a meadow. Though much of it was illumined by the half-moon that hung low in the sky, large sections were obscured by clouds of smoke that rolled from a fire raging at the meadow's far side, almost as if light and dark themselves were battling for dominance. In that lurid mix of moonlight, firelight, and smoky shadow, Rajiv could see hundreds of men, unicorns, and delvers locked in ferocious combat. The boy watched, sickened, as one of the Hunters — not five paces from where he stood — slashed across a unicorn's chest with a shining sword. Blood, silvery-crimson, spurted out in a graceful arc. The unicorn, screaming, pummeled at the man with flashing silver hooves. One blow connected with the man's head. One was all it took. Rajiv heard a horrible, dull thud then saw the man fall. Trumpeting defiance, the wounded unicorn reared, its shining hooves pawing the smoky air, then bent sideways and collapsed on top of the fallen man, their blood mingling. The boy could not tell whether either of them was alive or dead.

He sprinted forward. Despite the times he had longed to be bigger, he now blessed his small size, which let him zigzag across the field largely unnoticed by man and unicorn alike. Each had greater dangers than a mere boy on which to concentrate. Even the delvers, who were about his size, were so focused on battling the unicorns that they largely ignored him.

The screams, the cries of pain and rage, pounded in his ears. The smell of blood and death sickened him. But he did not slow his pace. A few minutes later — minutes during which he saw more horrors than a lifetime on the streets of Delhi had shown him — he stood at the edge of a small village of tents. The ones farthest from him were aflame, a fire that was spreading rapidly. The tents were all alike save one, larger and far more grand, that stood at the center of the grouping. He made for it at once, thinking it the most likely place to find the sahib.

The front of the tent was open. The sight was tempting, but entering there seemed unwise. Despite the battle, despite the fire, it was possible the sahib was guarded. That assumed, of course, that this was actually where he was being held.

Rajiv circled to the back of the tent. To his annoyance, he could not lift its edge. The tent's walls were attached to its floor, as they had been in the one he had shared with the sahibs on their journey into the Himalayas. He drew his sword, thinking it was a very good thing that the sahibs had seen fit to arm him back at the castle. He looked at the blade for a moment, then wriggled out of his shirt and used it to wrap the razor-sharp edge. Once it was safe to clutch, he cautiously and quietly used the tip to make a tiny opening, cutting into the tent close to the ground level. He widened the hole a bit with his finger. Then, lying on his side, he peered in.

The sahib was bound to a pole in the center of the tent.

He was the only one there.

It would have been easy enough to return to the front of the tent now and enter that way. But Rajiv was not feeling kindly toward the sahib's captors. So he simply unwrapped his blade, slid back into his shirt, then sliced a boy-high opening into the canvas.

At the sounds, Ian struggled to turn to see what was happening, but his bonds held him too tightly to make it out. Then, a familiar voice whispered, "No need to fear, sahib. It is me, Rajiv. I have come to free you!"

The boy spoke the words softly, moving to the sahib as he did. Once beside him, he quickly sliced the gag that covered Ian's mouth. When the cloth fell away Ian whispered, "Rajiv! What are you doing here?"

"Oh, sahib! You did not think I would leave you in

such a situation, did you? Do not move. I am going to cut the ropes that bind you, and I do not want to hurt you."

It was the work of but a moment to saw through the bonds. With a cry of relief Ian tried to get to his feet, but staggered and fell.

"Sahib!"

"It's all right, Rajiv. I should not have tried to stand so quickly. My legs have fallen asleep. I just need a moment."

"We should not take even a moment. We must flee! Lean on me, and we will begin." But as they were leaving the grouping of tents, they stumbled over a body.

Ian looked down, then groaned.

"What is it, sahib?" asked Rajiv.

"Help me get him to his feet," replied Ian. "We have to take him with us."

24

THE WRESTLING MATCH

Luster: The Wilderness

L izard and his cove stood outside a small clearing. The space within was nearly dark, the half-moon's light blocked by the towering trees that surrounded them. This was no problem for the delvers, whose eyes were made for such conditions. They could see everything quite clearly. And what they saw now was Fallon, who stood in the center of the clearing, stripped to the waist.

Stretching out his powerful arms, the big man roared, "I call you, Whisperer! I call and command, as you are bound to me by the fact that you came from the creatures I created. Appear to me. *Appear to me!*"

"What is he doing?" asked Pebble breathlessly.

Before Lizard could answer, a voice seemed to come from nowhere. Though soft, it somehow filled the clearing, whispering in seductive tones, "Why don't we just talk instead?"

The delvers looked at each other uneasily. They had not wanted to believe Rocky's horrible story, but this had to be the voice he had spoken of, the whispering voice that had driven their king mad. And if that were so, then perhaps the rest of the story was true and this Whisperer really had put part of itself into a tribe of dwarves, and from them created the delvers. And if *that* were so, he was both their creator and, in a way, their destroyer.

Lizard heard a sniffle and turned to glare at Waterfall. Wiping at his face, the delver nodded and fell silent.

"APPEAR TO ME!" roared Fallon again, his voice overpowering the noise of the not-too-distant battle.

A chuckle came from the air. "Do you really think that just because we are linked you can command me?"

"APPEAR TO ME!"

A sigh rustled through the clearing. A moment later a mist formed in front of Fallon. At first it was little more than slowly swirling tendrils, dark and murky, of a vile color.

"You cannot think to defeat me," purred the mist, as it curled around itself. "I am of you and of your creatures, but magnified a thousand times. So I am far better, and far stronger, than you could ever dream of being."

Now the watching delvers clung to one another. Lizard wanted to bolt, but knew that if he did the others would follow. And this was the task they had been given by the leader of their cove: to be present at this intimate battle.

Fallon's next words were nearly as soft as those of the Whisperer's, yet somehow even more compelling. He did not shout, but simply said with power and authority, "As the creator of the unicorns, from which you were yourself created, I command you: Appear to me!"

The mist swirled faster, angrily winding into and around itself. Slowly, excruciatingly slowly, it took on shape and substance, revealing the form of a man like Fallon, but twisted somehow. This twisting was not merely physical, though it was clear that something about its almost-beautiful body was not quite right. No, it was twisted in all ways, an external indication of its internal wrongness.

"Appear to me," repeated Fallon, the command now given through gritted teeth.

With a cry of rage the Whisperer did just that, finally coalescing into a solid presence, its body almost that of a man yet warped out of all proportion, its

THE WRESTLING MATCH

face so distorted by anger and fear and greed and base desire that it was terrifying to see.

"So," said Fallon, gazing at it sadly, "you are the worst of me."

"Of you and from you," replied the Whisperer maliciously.

"I reject you, utterly."

The malformed face twisted as it sneered and said, "Reject your own heart then, for I am born and built from its darker parts."

Fallon stared at the Whisperer as if looking into some evil mirror. Finally he smiled grimly and said, "I correct myself. I do not reject you. I simply claim what is mine . . . claim it — and conquer it!"

With that, he launched himself at the Whisperer. Their bodies struck with a meaty smack, making it clear that the Whisperer was now fully carnate.

In the first moments, Fallon seemed to have the advantage, by virtue of surprise more than strength. The Whisperer staggered backward, until it fell against a tree. Fallon pressed forward, pinning his counterpart to the bark. But just as it looked as if the battle might be over almost before it began, the Whisperer emitted an unearthly scream and flung Fallon away. The big man struck the ground with a jolt that drove the breath from his lungs. Before he could catch it again, the Whisperer hurled itself upon him.

Now began a long, strange time as the two powerful beings grappled on the forest floor. From moment to moment the watching delvers could not tell who was winning and who losing. The wrestlers rolled and cursed, shouted and shrieked, first one on top and then the other, one pinned and breaking free, then the other doing the same.

As Fallon and the Whisperer rolled across the leaf-strewn ground, which bucked and trembled beneath them, the cove stood in silence, scarcely able to breathe. They broke their silence to shriek cries of warning when the two wrestlers rolled to the edge of a suddenly opened fissure that might easily swallow both of them.

"This might make a good ending," crooned the Whisperer as he and Fallon struggled at the edge of the abyss. "We can disappear into that darkness together. Who knows where it might lead? To a new world? To oblivion? I don't mind dying, as long as I can take you with me!" With those words the creature dug its heels into the soil and began using them as leverage to push closer to the expanding gap.

Fallon made no answer, only a groan of effort as he tightened his grip on his intimate enemy. The straining muscles of his arms bulged as if they might burst through his skin. With a sudden roar, he flipped the Whisperer and they rolled back to solid ground. Locked in their deadly embrace, they tumbled over and over each other until they smashed against the twisting roots of one of the great trees. Fallon's head struck the root with an impact that left him momentarily dazed. The Whisperer took advantage of this

THE WRESTLING MATCH

and with a sudden twist pinned its enemy. Pressing the advantage, the twisted creature wrapped its hands around Fallon's throat and began to choke him, slowly closing its powerful fingers on the muscular neck.

Fallon fought desperately, but could not dislodge his opponent. The Whisperer bent toward him. "Did you really think you could defeat me?" it hissed, squeezing its hands still tighter.

Fallon beat his own hands against the ground, then twitched and lay still.

"Noooo!" screamed Lizard.

Without thinking, the delver raced into the clearing. The rest of his cove followed close at his heels. "This is for what you did to us!" Lizard shrieked as he jabbed his spear at the Whisperer. "And this . . . and this . . . and THIS!" cried the others, as they joined in.

Bellowing in astonished fury, the Whisperer turned and struck out at them, sending Wart and Diamond flying.

That moment of relief was all Fallon needed. He sucked in a gasping breath, then with one smooth flip of his body reversed the situation and pinned the Whisperer.

"Stand back," he rasped to the delvers.

They did as he commanded.

The Whisperer writhed beneath him, spitting, clawing, shrieking furious curses. Then, suddenly, it lay still and whispered, "Have mercy on me. You are wise and powerful. Oh, have mercy, my creator, for you are the source of all that I am."

Fallon said nothing, simply stared into the creature's eyes, a long, searching gaze filled with horror and compassion. Finally after what seemed to the watching delvers an eternity, he leaned down and kissed his dark twin on the forehead. Whispering now himself, he said, "All right, at last I know you. That is what I needed."

Then, with a wrenching movement that made his muscles bulge, he tore away a piece of the Whisperer's shoulder.

"This is for my *alahim*," he growled as he flung the piece skyward. The Whisperer screamed as the bloodless flesh arced upward, then spread out and . . . vanished.

Fallon tore off another piece of the creature's flesh and again flung it toward the stars, this time crying, "And this is for my unicorns!"

Again the Whisperer screamed.

Again the flesh expanded, dissipated, vanished.

"Mercy!" pleaded the Whisperer. "Oh, show me mercy!"

"So you can destroy more lives?" cried Fallon.

The Whisperer was writhing in his grip now, raking the big man's arms with fingers that still had uncanny strength. It had no effect. Fallon simply clasped his foe even closer and, his own voice now little more than a whisper, said simply, "You are of me, and from me, and I shall see to your ending."

Then he ripped away another piece of the coalesced darkness.

THE WRESTLING MATCH

"This," he said fiercely, "*this* is for the delvers that you corrupted!"

Slowly, surely, with every ounce of strength left to him, Fallon continued the dismemberment, pulling apart the Whisperer until nothing remained but the still-beating heart. He moved as if to fling this away, too, then sighed wearily. Turning toward Lizard, he said, "This ending must be sealed, or the creature might yet reassemble itself."

With those words, Fallon pressed the last remnant of the Whisperer to his own chest. The still-beating heart blazed with dark fire for a moment, then disappeared as, with a cry of torment, Fallon took back into himself some of his own darkness.

He heaved a deep sigh. Then, murmuring, "It is finished!" he collapsed in a dead stupor.

Lizard nodded to the others. Swiftly they gathered around Fallon's beautiful body, which was now scored with dozens of wounds and streaked with silvery blood.

Without speaking, and in perfect coordination, they lifted him and carried him into the darkness.

25

ON FIELD OF BATTLE

Luster: Beloved's Encampment

Their screams alone are enough to make your blood run cold, thought Amalia as she watched Gnurflax and his delvers pour onto the field of battle.

Small and fast, screeching a fierce ululation, the little monsters darted among the unicorns. Scarcely knee high to the unicorns, the delvers jabbed up at their bellies with spears, tangled their feet in nets, tripped them with ropes. Blood flowed and cries of panic filled the air.

Yet despite the ferocity of the delver attacks, Feng Yuan thought to the Queen in astonishment, "They are holding back!"

"What do you mean?" asked Amalia.

"For some reason, the delvers have the same problem as your unicorns. Look at how fiercely they fight. Yet despite that, most are not going for the kill."

"Thank goodness for that," replied Amalia grimly. "But why?"

Rather than answer, the girl asked, "What are those flashes of light?"

"I believe it is my friend, Thomas the Tinker. He specializes in minor explosions."

"A very useful friend," replied Feng Yuan. "But I wish I knew what was happening with our other presumed friend, the lady Firethroat. Where has she gone?"

Though she had no answer for this question, the Queen replied, "Trust her. I certainly do."

The dreadful scene spread before them was lit by a strange mix of moonlight and the ghastly orange glow of burning tents. In places, the light was blocked by dark swirls of smoke. The acrid scent now reached all the way across the meadow.

The delvers' arrival had given heart to the Hunters, who raised a cry of triumph and began to fight the unicorns more brutally than ever.

The Queen groaned.

"But look at Belle!" thought Feng Yuan with pride. "She is doing her best to rally *our* forces!"

Indeed, Belle, the fiercest of the unicorns, seemed to be everywhere at once, racing from one melee to another, striking at Hunters, using her teeth to wrench an arrow or spear from the side of a wounded but still-standing unicorn, aiming her back hooves in sudden kicks that sent Hunters flying. Her clear voice rose above the battle as she shouted encouragement everywhere she went.

Which was why the Hunters, the ones who realized what she was doing, decided to concentrate on her.

"Look!" thought Feng Yuan in alarm, pointing toward a group of Hunters who had clearly recognized Belle as one of the unicorn leaders. The men had formed a wedge and were pushing their way through the battle, obviously intending to strike her down.

"We have to help her!"

"You have cautioned me repeatedly that it is folly for a general to join the battle proper," replied the Queen.

"I have changed my mind! It may not be wise, My Queen, but tonight I say wisdom be damned. I have only a dagger, but even one blade can sway a battle. I say let us fight!"

"Let us fight!" trumpeted Amalia. She reared and pawed the air, then planted her feet solidly on the shaking ground. Swiftly Feng Yuan scrambled onto the Queen's back. Together they galloped into the fray.

Feng Yuan longed to shout, "To the Queen, to the Queen!" But she knew none of the unicorns would understand her. She need not have worried. Cloudmane started the cry on her own. "Fight for Luster! Fight for the Queen! Fight for your lives!!"

Because of her connection to Amalia, Feng Yuan could understand the unicorn's shouts and saw the results as several unicorns picked up the call and rallied to their side.

Belle, unaware of her danger, had reared and was pummeling a pair of delvers who cut at her with their spears. As Amalia drew closer, Feng Yuan was horrified to see what had been invisible to her from farther off: Streams of crimson and silver blood flowed along Belle's heaving flanks.

The approaching Hunters, most carrying swords but two with spears, were only a few feet away now. One of the spearmen flung his weapon. It lodged in Belle's shoulder. With a cry of defiance she bent her neck and wrenched the thing out. Doing so loosed an arc of blood that spattered on the delvers she had been battling. The other spearman raised his weapon — and fell beneath the hooves of five unicorns, led by Amalia Flickerfoot.

Feng Yuan leaped from Amalia's back, onto the back of one of the Hunters. He staggered, and she twisted, throwing him further off balance, so that he fell to the ground. She sprang away. A unicorn did the rest. . . .

She was heading for the Queen when another Hunter grabbed her and spun her around. To her horror, she found herself staring into the eyes of her old teacher, Wu Chen.

"Oh, Feng Yuan!" he cried. "That you would betray us so!"

"Master, you don't understand!"

"I understand treachery," he said. Tears filling his own eyes, he raised his sword to kill her. The blade whistled toward her, but before it could reach her flesh Belle struck from behind, crushing his skull. A wail burst from Feng Yuan as he crumpled to the ground, for Wu Chen had been her true teacher and had taught her the ways of war.

She caught her breath and straightened her shoulders. *Such is the way of war,* she thought. Then she raised her dagger and flung herself on the nearest Hunter.

The Maidens of the Hunt, who had returned to the main encampment with their Hunters, had fled their tents. Some were screaming and near delirium. Others, more well-trained, had searched for weapons and were racing past the blazing tents to join the fight.

Beloved was observing the battle from one of her watchtowers. Dark smoke snaked around her as the tents burned. Suddenly she stretched her arms to the pitch black sky and cried, "Where are you? Friend Whisperer, where are you? How could you abandon me now of all times?"

No answer came from the darkness.

Drawing a deep breath, she spat into her hands, then rolled air between them until she had a glowing ball of red light. She hurled it at the closest unicorn. It struck him in the chest. He reared, trumpeting in pain as the blazing light enveloped him, burning at his skin. Screaming with agony, he collapsed, hitting the ground with a thud.

Beloved's shout of triumph was cut off when she felt her knees buckle. She cursed herself for giving way to her frustration. She knew very well that the kind of magic she had just used drew too much power. She would need time to recover before she could launch another such blast.

Still, the painful death of that unicorn had been satisfying to watch.

As she leaned against the rail of the watchtower, trying to regain her strength, a coil of smoke made her cough. Looking down, she saw that flames were licking at the tower's base. With a cry of panic, she began to descend the ladder.

The flames stretched for her scarlet robe. . . .

With Feng Yuan once more clinging to her back, Amalia galloped across the smoky field, rallying her troops. Suddenly they saw Moonheart. Hooves flashing in the moonlight, the big unicorn was battling three delvers and a pair of Hunters. An arrow protruded from his right shoulder, and blood flowed from a gash on his side. Behind him lay the plump form of Armando de la Quintano. The man was wounded and struggling to rise, and Moonheart was protecting him.

Despite his wounds, the big unicorn was fighting with full force. Before Amalia could reach his side he had struck down the closest Hunter and disabled two of the delvers. But just as Amalia thought he would be safe she saw a well-placed spear pierce Moonheart's chest. With a shriek he crashed to his side. He struggled to rise, then fell back, flailing his hooves and bellowing in rage.

"Brother!" cried Amalia.

Screaming in fury, the Queen leaped forward. With vengeful hooves, she dashed the Hunter whose spear had struck Moonheart to the ground, then trampled him.

Feng Yuan could not hold on to the Queen's back while this happened. But she landed lightly and turned to slash at an approaching delver.

And, moment by moment, the shaking and heaving of the ground beneath them grew more violent.

26

TO THE TREE!

Luster: Near the Axis Mundi

In the forest near the Axis Mundi, not yet aware of the battle raging in the southwest meadow, Lightfoot said to Martha, "It is easy enough to guess where Rajiv has gone. He is deeply attached to Ian. Once he knew your husband had been captured, he would not be interested in any stories being told here. I'm sure he is heading for Beloved's camp to try to free him."

"We have to go after him," said Martha. She was still clinging to Cara's neck but had one hand on Lightfoot's shoulder as well.

Lightfoot shook his head. "Rajiv might slip past any

guards they have, but I cannot enter that camp, nor can Cara, nor can you."

"But what are we to do?"

Rocky, who was standing nearby, asked what the problem was. After Cara explained, he said, "I can go. Since the delvers and the Hunters are now allies, I may be able to enter the camp. I doubt the Hunters are aware that I am an exile."

"Why would you risk this?" asked Cara.

"Your father saved my life not long ago. I am in his debt."

Martha, who received this information through her connection with Cara and Lightfoot, said urgently, "Please do!"

"It will be faster if you ride on my back," said Lightfoot. "I can take you to the edge of their encampment, then let you go forward on your own."

"You would do that?" asked Rocky. "Let me, a delver, ride you?"

Lightfoot grimaced. "I will not pretend the idea does not give me shivers. But the whole world is shivering now. Everything is changing. I can, too."

"Then let us go!"

Lightfoot knelt and Rocky climbed onto his back. No sooner had he done so than both unicorn and delver cried out in surprise.

"What's wrong?" asked Cara.

Lightfoot shook his head. "I can't say that something is wrong. It's just that as Rocky climbed on I felt a strange charge of energy. Not bad . . . just strange."

TO THE TREE!

Rocky, who had a bewildered expression on his face, said, "And I felt a calming, as if some uneasiness that has been with me all my life was quieted."

"Fascinating," said Lightfoot. "Alas, we have no time to try to understand what it means. Let's go!"

With that he galloped into the woods.

"Yaahhh!" cried Rocky. Leaning forward, he clutched Lightfoot's neck, trying desperately not to fall off.

Across the writhing meadow, M'Gama stood at the base of the Axis Mundi, staring at the tree with bleak despair. Namza, who was at her side, pointed up and said, "What is that odd piece of wood embedded in the trunk?"

"It is a chunk of rootwood, from one of the great trees that grow at the center of the unicorns' seasonal resting places. I was using it — I had a piece from each of those trees — to cast a protective spell. Unfortunately, I was captured before I could finish."

Namza sighed. "For that I am sorry. But do not think your work was in vain, M'Gama. I can tell that, had you not done this, the tree would have split already and with that, ended our world. Now we must do what we can to try to hold things together."

"I thought you said you could not heal the tree?"

"And that is, alas, the truth. To do that would require a magic far beyond my own. The best we can do is try to stave off the last moments and hope for a miracle. Let us go into the ground and see if we can soothe these troubled roots."

Lying side by side at the base of the tree, their bodies tossed by the constant shifting of the tormented roots, the stone wizards joined first hands, then magics. Leaving their bodies behind, they sank into the trembling ground to try to hold off the end of the world.

Despite the Queen's entry into the battle, which gave the unicorns new resolve, they were losing ground.

We fought valiantly, even if we have lost, thought the Queen. Then she stamped her foot and recalled the words she had so often spoken to Cara during the days that she, Amalia, was a human: *If you're alive, you have a chance.* With a defiant cry, she charged once more into the fray. But even as she shot forward Feng Yuan cried, "Look! Oh, look, My Queen!"

Amalia turned in the direction the girl was pointing and cried out in joy.

Firethroat had returned! Wings spread wide, the massive dragon swooped low over the battle. She made a quick dive and snatched up a Hunter. She reversed course, flew up for about a hundred feet, then dropped him.

He fell screaming to his death.

New chaos erupted on the battlefield. And into that chaos charged the centaurs that Firethroat had flown off to fetch, the band of warriors she had misdirected earlier that day, before she knew the Queen's true plan.

TO THE TREE!

Towering over all the combatants, Arkon and his troops — fifty-one centaurs in all, fresh and eager for the fight — thundered onto the field, whooping their savage war cries. Some were wielding swords. Some hefted spears. Some clutched bows with arrows nocked and ready to fly. A few of them swung double-headed axes so sharp-edged they could slice flesh just by touching it.

Princess Arianna, fighting near the center of the field, cried out in joy at the sight of her fellow centaurs charging into the battle. Despite the wounds she had taken, and the arrows in her flank, she trampled two men beneath her in her eagerness to join them.

"Arkon!" she cried, rushing forward.

He turned and shouted her name. In that same moment a Hunter's arrow struck her directly in the chest.

Arianna reared back with a scream. Defiantly, she grasped the arrow then ripped it from her breast and charged forward.

She managed three steps before she stumbled and fell.

With a roar, Arkon fought his way toward her, slicing at Hunters with his sword as he trampled delvers beneath his oversized hooves.

The glow of the burning tents was lurid as Ian Hunter bent to help up the man over whom he had nearly fallen.

"Who is it, sahib?" asked Rajiv.

"A friend of my wife's family," replied Ian, not taking the time to explain that Jacques might actually be his wife's father. Once he had the old man's arm around his neck — Jacques was conscious, but just barely — Ian said, "Take the lead, Rajiv. How do we get out of here?"

Before the boy could answer, Jacques's legs buckled, nearly pulling Ian down. Rajiv immediately moved to the man's other side. He lifted the man's hand and placed it on his shoulder. "All right, sahib," he said. "We'll go this way."

Ian groaned.

"What is it, sahib?"

"You will have to be my eyes, Rajiv. I have lost my sight again."

The boy nodded, realized that was useless, and shouted, "You hired me to be your guide, sahib. I am glad to continue." Brushing away a bit of burning canvas, he began to lead the two men out of the inferno. They staggered forward. What else was there to do?

Beloved's robes had caught fire as she scrambled to escape the burning watchtower. Silently she leaped from the ladder and rolled upon the ground. Though serious burns scored her body, she was no stranger to pain and did not let it stop her now. She stripped off her outer robe and strode toward the battle, pausing only to pull a sword from the body of one of her

TO THE TREE!

Hunters. Swinging it once, she vowed she would draw blood on her own before this was done.

A sudden roar attracted her attention. She pivoted to her right, then cried out in fury. Even from where she stood, on the far side of the battlefield from where they entered, it was easy to spot the centaurs, since they towered above everyone else in the fray.

"No!" screamed Beloved as she watched them gallop into the battle. "No, this cannot be!"

The arrival of the centaurs was too much for the Hunters, and their ranks began to break.

"To the tree!" cried one of them. "To the tree and back to Earth! This is madness!"

"To the tree!" cried another, and then another.

Their cries began to swell. Suddenly, as if seized by a rapidly spreading infection, Beloved's army turned and moved into full retreat, plunging into the forest that surrounded the battlefield.

With a cry of triumph the unicorns gave chase.

Screaming in rage, Beloved bolted after them.

Behind them, the site of the first battle ever fought in Luster was strewn with the bodies of Hunters, unicorns, delvers, and one centaur.

Some of the fallen were alive, but too badly wounded to be able to rise and run.

Others would never rise again.

Beside one of those who would never rise, a female centaur of uncommon beauty, knelt the newly named Chiron. He held her close in his powerful arms. She lifted a cold hand to stroke his cheek. "You came," she whispered. "You came, you came! Oh, Arkon, I knew you would not fail me."

He drew her close, pressed her to his chest. "Arianna!"

"I have to leave you now," she whispered. "Forgive me, my love."

"No!" he screamed. He pulled her still closer and buried his face in her chestnut hair.

Breathing her last, Arianna collapsed in his loving embrace.

Arkon continued to hold her as heaving sobs wracked his chest. At last he lowered her carefully to the ground. Rising, he hurled a defiant cry of grief to the smoke-smeared sky. Then he turned and thundered into the woods, in pursuit of the fleeing Hunters.

27

DRAGON BINDING

Luster: Above the Axis Mundi

Because the forest through which the Hunters fled was too dense for dragonflight, Graumag and Firethroat went above it. As a consequence, the two dragons arrived at the Axis Mundi well ahead of the fleeing Hunters. But as they swooped over the meadow surrounding the great tree they saw — could not help but see — a heart-stopping sight: The ragged gap that Beloved had opened at the tree's base now extended up the vast trunk for hundreds of feet. The upper branches were trembling, and it was clear the tree would soon split, sending its gigantic halves crashing to the ground.

"If the tree splits, all is finished!" cried Graumag.

"If the tree splits, Luster dies," agreed Firethroat.

No more needed to be said. Both dragons knew what must be done. It was a temporary solution and could not last for long. But moments, seconds, counted right now. Without another word, they dove toward the dividing tree, then attached themselves to the trunk some hundred and fifty feet above the ground.

Moving quickly, and with remarkable grace, the dragons wound themselves around the wood, overlapping each other until that section of the tree looked like a giant caduceus, the ancient symbol of healing still used by Earth's physicians. Once the intertwining was complete, the dragons twisted the tips of their tails together, then stretched around the trunk to join claws.

"I do not know how long I can hold on," gasped Graumag, who was the smaller of the two.

"Nor do I," replied Firethroat. "I do not even know if there is any reason to do so. This tree is dying, and I see no hope of saving it. But what else shall we do? Die on the ground, doing nothing as Luster perishes? Let it not be said that you and I failed to battle against the end of the world until the last moment. Persist, sister. Persist!"

Her words were answered by a groan of anguish from Graumag: "I feel as if I am being torn apart!"

Firethroat tightened her grip on Graumag's legs. "Hold fast! *Hold fast!*"

But she could feel the tree pressing out against them, its great weight threatening to pull them apart.

Soon Firethroat, too, cried out — first in pain, then defiance. "I will hold on! Past pain, past agony, I will hold until the tree itself rips me asunder!"

Graumag's answering scream was wordless, yet Firethroat knew her Flame Sister was making the same promise.

And still the wounded tree pressed against them, the slow creak of its splitting wood like a vast scream of its own.

28

AT THE CENTER

Luster: The Axis Mundi

The Dimblethum had been lurking in the forest that surrounded the meadow of the great tree. He was confused and unhappy, but did not know what to do. All he really understood was that he had done something bad and then tried to make up for it by doing something good. After that, everything had gone all hazy again.

He flexed his great claws, wishing there was something he could tear apart. Not the trees, though. He loved the trees, the Big Tree most of all. But that one was in trouble. The hole in its center was growing. Its roots were twisting and its branches shaking. He feared it was dying, and his longing to fix it was so intense that it was like a knife in his heart.

But he had no idea how to do it.

He growled angrily. Why couldn't he ever make something without it going bad?

Suddenly he heard shouts and cries and screams coming in his direction. The sounds made him want to hide. Not out of fear. The Dimblethum did not fear things. He simply wanted to be alone. He ran to the left, circling trees and leaping over exposed roots. It did no good . . . the cries were still coming. He reversed course and ran right, but heard more shouts and screams from that direction. He groaned. Was no place free of these invaders?

A moment later he saw the men. He knew they were called Hunters.

The Dimblethum remembered that he did not like Hunters.

And he was unhappy.

This combination was not a good thing for the Hunters.

Lightfoot and Rocky had nearly made it through the forest to Beloved's encampment when they were startled to see a flood of men and delvers surging toward them. Among them, all clad in white, ran the Maidens of the Hunt. Lightfoot could feel the unwanted surge of desire to help them, but fought it down.

THE GATHERED GLORY

Behind the men and the maidens, driving them forward, were the unicorns of Luster, beautiful in their fury, glorious in their power. With them ran dozens of centaurs, brandishing spears and swords and rending the air with savage war cries. Behind them came the men of Sweetwater, swinging their farming implements with deadly intent.

Lightfoot longed to join this chase, but he had promised to help find Cara's father. So with Rocky still clinging to his neck, the Prince veered sideways to avoid the first flow of the Hunters. Ignoring brambles, nimbly leaping over roots and cracks in the surface, he raced parallel to the oncoming Hunters, but in the opposite direction, back toward the field of battle.

It didn't take long to reach the abandoned meadow. But the dreadful sight that greeted them there — so many wounded, so many dead — nearly drove Lightfoot to his knees. But grieving would have to wait. He headed across the body-strewn field, picking his way among the fallen, until one familiar form caught his eye — and his heart.

"Moonheart!" he wailed.

Now he did fall to his knees. Ignoring Rocky's protests that he could not afford to attempt a healing now, he pressed his horn to his uncle's side. His heart went cold when he realized no energy would flow from him to the fallen warrior.

Unicorns can heal, but they cannot resurrect.

AT THE CENTER

Staggering to his feet, half-blinded by tears of rage and grief, the Prince forced himself to move on toward the still-blazing tents.

The forest floor bucked and heaved as the Hunters fled toward the Axis Mundi. The quakes — "tremors" was no longer a sufficient word, the world was clearly tearing itself apart — were growing stronger and more frequent than ever.

Passage through the woods was difficult. Everyone involved in that desperate chase — man or woman, delver, unicorn, or centaur — was repeatedly knocked to the ground. Far more terrifying, new fissures continued to open in the forest floor, some directly at the feet of the runners. The cries of those who could not turn fast enough, but instead fell in, were terrifying.

On the far side of the Axis Mundi, seven delvers also made their way through the forest toward the meadow. They traveled single file, arms upraised, bearing the unconscious body of Fallon. The trip would not have been difficult — he was big, but surprisingly light for his size — if not for the wretched heaving of the ground.

At least, thought Lizard, *we haven't fallen into any crevices.* After another spasm in the forest floor he added the thought, *Well, at least, not yet.*

It was obvious the danger of that was growing worse. So he was relieved when a beautiful voice said, "Let me take your burden, delver."

Cara and her mother had braved the meadow's upheavals and were making their way to the tree, which now appeared to be surrounded by an odd band of calm. They both had the same idea, but in each case it was for the other.

"You should go through the tree right now," urged Cara as they approached. "You can get back to Earth where it's safe."

"Not without your father," replied Martha firmly. "But you should go now. I want you out of this."

"And what would I do on Earth as a unicorn? I can't live there. Luster is my world now." She paused, then added to herself, *At least, for as long as it lasts.*

They heard a shout from behind, turned, and saw a row of men approaching. The first wave of Hunters had arrived. Though their progress was slowed by the meadow's ever-worsening disruptions, their intent was made clear by the man in front, who bellowed, "By god, I'll get one more unicorn before I go!"

Drawing his sword, he rushed toward Cara.

Stepping in front of her daughter, Martha Hunter also drew her sword.

* * *

AT THE CENTER

As the flames devouring Beloved's camp grew more intense, Rajiv began to question whether he could manage to lead Ian and the old man Ian was carrying out of the inferno. Just as despair was about to overwhelm him, Lightfoot came galloping out of the smoke.

The boy had to fight from dropping to his knees in relief. "It is good you came, Sahib Lightfoot," he said, placing a soot-smeared hand on Lightfoot's shoulder. "Sahib Hunter and I were having a hard time with the old sahib. I do not think we could get him back to the others without your help."

"Thank you for coming, Prince," said Ian, who was supporting Jacques' limp body with one arm while he placed his right hand on Lightfoot's other shoulder.

"I'm here, too," said Rocky, sounding offended.

Ian sighed. "Forgive me, friend delver. I cannot see right now, and . . ."

"Cannot see?" cried Rocky.

"It will pass," said Ian. "But I will need help until my sight returns."

Just then the older man groaned and rolled his head.

"It's Jacques!" thought Lightfoot, seeing the man's face for the first time. "Is he in mortal danger?"

"I don't think so," replied Ian, "though he would have been, had Rajiv not rescued me. We found him among the burning tents as we began our escape. I think he just needs time to recover."

"Then it would be better for me to carry him than

try to heal him, since that would leave me unable to walk myself."

"That makes sense. Thank you for being willing to do that. I do not want my wife to miss the chance to meet this man."

"Nor would Amalia Flickerfoot ever forgive me if I let him perish here," replied Lightfoot. "Let us try to get back to the center. We may have a chance for one last good-bye before the world falls to pieces."

The Dimblethum was lost in his rage against the Hunters, the latest and most destructive of Luster's invaders. He had quickly dispatched four of them when the first wave of the fleeing men had reached him. Now he pursued them into the meadow, stumbling and staggering across the troubled ground, bellowing in anguish for his wounded world. Most Hunters and delvers simply fled before him, terrified by his size and ferocity. A few turned to fight. Those battles were brief, and the Dimblethum quickly flung aside their battered, broken bodies. Still, these victories did not come without a price; he was bleeding now from a score of wounds.

It made no difference. His despair was complete, and nothing made a difference now.

At least, not until a voice that sounded oddly familiar, the voice of someone he cared for, called his name.

* * *

AT THE CENTER

Untrained in the use of the sword, Martha Hunter would have been at a huge disadvantage if not for the wild gyrations of the meadow. As the ground bucked and heaved no one, no matter how skilled, could hold steady, parry a blow, strike with confidence. Two more Hunters followed the first; more were following after them. When the lead Hunter was only a few feet from Martha, he thrust his blade toward her. She countered the move, but in a flash he knocked the sword from her hand. He laughed at the look on her face, then pushed past her to attack her daughter.

The mockery died on his lips when the smaller blade that Martha carried in her boot found a home in his back.

Cara was battering at another Hunter with her hooves. She struck him a glancing blow, destroying his shoulder, before she was knocked to the ground by an upward surge of the meadow. Screaming with pain, the man flung himself toward her. Martha did the same, shouting, "Don't touch my daughter!" She wrapped her arm around the Hunter's throat and began choking him with a strength she had not known she possessed. He pulled and scratched at her arm. She spotted a fallen arrow, snatched it up, and thrust it into his neck. He gasped and fell from her grip.

Cara struggled to her feet. Three more Hunters were approaching, blades drawn. As the first lunged toward her, she heard a fierce shriek from above.

"Gaaaah!"

Looking up, she saw Medafil plunge from the sky.

Talons outstretched, a mighty roar bursting from his throat, the gryphon raked his claws across the face of one of the Hunters. As the man screamed and fell to his knees, Medafil sank his beak into the shoulder of another. The Hunter flailed at him with his free hand, but Medafil flew upward, just as Firethroat had done with the Hunter she had plucked from the battlefield. But Medafil was much smaller than the dragon, and the man's struggles caused the gryphon to falter and lose his hold.

The Hunter would have landed safely, had he not managed to squirm free of the Medafil's grip directly above a widening crevice.

His cry of terror went on long after he had disappeared from sight.

A volley of arrows flew in Medafil's direction as more Hunters entered the field. Most were badly aimed because no one could take a firm stance, and the gryphon ignored them at first. Then a lucky shot burst through his right wing, sending big feathers scattering. Medafil shrieked in outrage, but managed to keep flying.

Another arrow struck, and then another.

"Gaaaah!" he cried as he fell to the shaking ground. Ragged wing limp at this side, he surged to his feet. "Do your worst you frib-jabbled Hunters. I will slice you till my last breath!"

* * *

AT THE CENTER

Most of those who had survived the flight through the forest had made it to the meadow by this time. The restless surface was nearly covered by a surging mass of men and delvers, unicorns and centaurs.

The men were running for the tree.

"They're fleeing!" thought Feng Yuan, who was still clinging to Amalia Flickerfoot's back. The two were in the first wave of the unicorns to reach the meadow. "Press the advantage, My Queen. Drive them out!"

"Drive them out!" trumpeted Amalia. "Drive the Hunters out of Luster!"

It was hard to be heard above the shouts of the men, the screams of the dragons, the rumbling and grinding of the splitting world. Even so, the unicorns nearest to the Queen took up the call: "Drive them out! Drive the Hunters out of Luster!"

Across the field spread the rallying cry: "Drive them out! Drive the Hunters out of Luster!"

King Gnurflax had been seized by the bloodlust that can come in battle. The group of delvers he now led across the meadow attacked anyone they could reach, unicorn or Hunter, without distinction. Beloved had destroyed Delvharken. The Whisperer had abandoned him. To the berserk king, everyone — *everyone* — was now the enemy.

As his band of delvers fought their way toward the center, Gnurflax spotted a particularly tempting trio: a gryphon, a unicorn, and a human, all standing together.

"That way!" he cried.

Screaming their battle cry, the delvers sprang from behind, swarming over Cara, Medafil, and Martha.

Martha bellowed curses and fought like a madwoman.

Medafil struck out with beak and talons, snapping and clawing with the fury of a cornered beast.

The majority of the delvers went for Cara. She bucked and kicked as she tried to shake them off, but there were too many, and their battle lust had doubled their strength. Trumpeting defiance, Cara toppled sideways. As she fell she spotted a hulking figure. He was looking around at the chaos as if he did not know what to make of it. "Dimblethum!" she cried desperately. "Dimblethum, it's me, Cara! Help me! Help —"

Her plea was cut off by a delver pinning her head to the ground. But at her call the Dimblethum had turned. He hurled himself toward the fray, roaring as he came.

Delvers flew left and right as he plucked them from Cara's side. Some screamed as he flung them into the air, heedless of where they might fall. Others cried out in agony as he stomped them beneath his mighty feet.

The delvers turned from Martha and Medafil. Here was their great enemy!

"Kill him!" cried Gnurflax. "Kill the Dimblethum!"

They swarmed over him.

Bellowing in rage, the Dimblethum yanked the attackers from his body. They clung like leeches and took chunks of flesh with them, but in the blood haze that now possessed the Dimblethum such wounds meant nothing.

The world rumbled and shook again. The Dimblethum staggered and fell, crushing two delvers beneath his great bulk. Cara, Martha, and Medafil threw themselves back into the fight, trying to drag the little monsters away from the great beast battling on their behalf.

Cara felt a strange elation as she used her wonderful new body in ways she had not known possible. Silvery hooves flashing, she struck down delver after delver. When one leaped onto her back, she twisted her lithe neck and gripped his arm in her powerful jaws. She heard him scream, felt the bone break. With another twist of her neck, she wrenched him into the air, then sent him flying. He landed at the edge of a newly opened crevice and scrabbled wildly to avoid tumbling into its unknown depths.

As if their fellows' screams had alerted the delvers to how severe the quakes had become, they made a sudden retreat, leaving Cara standing alone, panting for breath, trying to keep her balance as the world continued to writhe around her. Turning, she saw that the Dimblethum was on his feet again. Gnurflax was clinging to the beast's great leg, which was like a small tree trunk. Stabbing at it with his stubby sword the delver king shrieked, "Die! Die, beast!"

Oddly, he was weeping as he did this.

The Dimblethum collapsed. Gnurflax, still weeping, leaped away from him, waving his sword in triumph.

Screaming in rage, Cara reared. With flailing hooves she rained a hail of silvery blows upon the delver king. He toppled beneath her onslaught and rolled away.

As he did, the ground opened and swallowed him.

The rest of the delvers fled, wailing in fear and despair.

29
TRANSFORMATIONS

Luster: The Axis Mundi

A strange silence had fallen over the meadow. It was not a complete silence. The shifting ground continued its ominous and ever-worsening rumbling. Firethroat and Graumag still shrieked with the pain of holding the tree together. But the battle proper had ended. Most of the Hunters and the maidens had fled through the tree. The ones left were too wounded to travel across the tortured and riven meadow and did not pose an immediate danger. One maiden lay crumpled at the base of the tree, as if her strength had run out before she could make the final sprint into the tunnel. Her white robes covered her like a shroud.

THE GATHERED GLORY

Though the enemy had fled, the greatest threat remained: Luster was about to rip itself apart. Yet the knoll surrounding the tree was oddly peaceful. This untroubled patch, which extended about twenty feet out from the trunk, was the work of Namza and M'Gama, whose bodies lay nearby. Their true selves were woven into the soil, working to calm the great tree's troubled roots. With the dragons binding the tree from above, and the wizards of earth and stone soothing the roots from below, the death of Luster was held off for at least a few more moments. But all four knew it was a delay, not a victory. The end was still coming.

As if in defiance of the approaching doom, the unicorns had spread back across the meadow and were moving from there to the main battlefield, in search of healing work. The Queen had ordered them to heal the unicorns first, but then, when possible, to turn their attention to others who had fallen that day, whether Hunter or delver. Hunters were to be healed with care, and only with at least two other unicorns at hand to keep them in control should they choose to attack.

Amalia Flickerfoot herself remained at the center, as it seemed the best place for her new seat of command, however briefly that command might last.

She had not been there long when into that circle of calmer ground stepped Allura. She was surrounded by seven delvers, who continually glanced up at her in awe. On her shoulder rode the Squijum. In her outstretched arms she carried Fallon's unconscious body.

TRANSFORMATIONS

"Awake, brother," she whispered. "You've earned your rest, but one last struggle remains."

She knew, and dreaded, the thing that must be done next — or, at least, attempted. She did not know if her brother had the strength for it, or if he did, if it was even truly possible.

"Awake, brother," she whispered again.

Fallon stirred and groaned. He looked at the tree and groaned again, the sound this time not one of physical pain, but of heart-deep despair.

As Allura helped her brother to his feet, she gasped. Fallon turned to see what had caught her attention.

They had been joined in the circle of peace by Ian, Martha, and Rajiv. With them were an old man, and the delver called Rocky. Behind the four humans and the delver, walking side by side and in perfect unison, were Prince Lightfoot and the unicorn that Fallon had come to know as Silverhoof, but who he now understood to be Ian Hunter's daughter, Cara.

Stretched across the backs of the two unicorns was the body of a creature that could only be the Dimblethum, the creature that had once been his *alahim* Elihu.

Fallon cried out in grief.

"He is not dead," said Ian, moving quickly to his friend's side. "But his wounds are severe."

The unicorns knelt. The Dimblethum rolled to the ground, where he lay upon his back, his eyes open but unseeing.

With two quick steps, Fallon crossed to his *alahim*. He looked down with sorrow at the wounded form of his oldest, dearest friend, then glanced at Cara. "You remember what I told you about Transformational Magic?"

Cara nodded.

"When Elihu transformed you into your unicorn self, he did so by passing to you the Transformational Magic with which the Whisperer had returned him to his true form."

Cara shuddered with guilt. Elihu had been as beautiful as Fallon. Now he was, again, simply . . . the Dimblethum. He had sacrificed his heart's desire to save her from the Hunters.

"Can I return the Transformational Magic and change him back?" she asked.

"Please try," said Fallon, and Cara caught the note of desperation in his voice. "We need him — he is the only one who can possibly stop the destruction of Luster."

Cara went to her dear friend and protector, the first being she had ever met in Luster. Now she could try to rescue him.

So many wounds! she thought, gazing down at him in sorrow. She remembered how fiercely he had resisted the first time she tried to heal him. Now she understood that it was because he did not want to let her return the Transformational Magic, though in his muddled state he might not even have completely understood that. Cara knelt and pressed her horn to his chest. Instantly she felt a surge of energy pour out of her.

So this is what a healing is like, she thought.

Yet she did not lose consciousness as she had seen happen with Lightfoot in the past.

The Dimblethum's breathing steadied. Some of his wounds healed. But he remained in his bestial form.

Fallon stepped beside her. "It is too late, Silverhoof," he said softly. "The Transformational Magic has been in you for too long. It has settled, and you do not have the knowledge to return it."

"Is there nothing to be done?" she cried in horror.

"Step aside," said Fallon.

Without another word, he straddled the Dimblethum's body. Reaching down, he grasped the great, brutish paws in his own hands, which — despite their size — were oddly delicate in comparison. He stared down at the bestial form of his *alahim,* then closed his eyes and began to murmur.

Light shimmered around them.

Fallon's face twisted and he cried out in pain. His body began to tremble, then shake violently.

The transformation began with Fallon's hands, which grew thick and coarse. His smooth arms sprouted dense fur. What was left of his clothing after his fight with the Whisperer tore away as his limbs grew thick and bulky. And his face . . .

Cara had to turn away as Fallon's once beautiful

face grew coarse and bestial, the jaw extending, the upper lip and straight nose merging to form a snout.

Allura was standing close, her face contorted by grief. Tears flowed down her cheeks.

Unable to resist, Cara turned back to the transformation and gasped yet again. The Dimblethum was changing in a way opposite to Fallon. His bearlike traits faded, his snout shrank, his fur vanished, until he was once more the exquisite Elihu.

From above, Cara could hear the screams of dragons. She wondered, vaguely, at the cause, but could not tear her eyes from the scene before her.

Finally the metamorphosis was complete. With a roar, Fallon wrenched his paws from Elihu's hands, then fell sideways. On the ground, he let out a gasping sob, a strange and horrible sound to hear coming from his hulking, bearlike body.

Elihu sat up. When he saw the new Dimblethum beside him he moaned in horror. "It's Fallon, isn't it?" he asked.

"Yes, my love," said Allura. "It is him."

Elihu extended his shapely hands toward his *alahim*.

"Don't!" cried Allura, before Elihu could actually touch the new Dimblethum. "If you make that connection the Transformational Magic will flow back to you. Fallon did this of his own free will, Elihu. He did it because . . . because you are needed here."

She gestured toward the tree.

Elihu turned and cried out when he saw the vast cleft that was destroying the tree, the tree that had grown from the seed he had stolen and then quickened with his own sacred blood.

"You have no time to waste," said Allura gently.

Elihu looked down at Fallon, and a sob choked in his throat. "Thank you, my friend," he murmured. "My *alahim*. Thank you for freeing me to do what must be done. Had I known this would be the end, that you would pay this price, I would never have begun."

All eyes had been riveted on the drama occurring between Fallon and Elihu. So no one had noticed when the white-clad figure lying at the base of the tree had risen.

No one had noticed when she crossed to join them.

No one noticed her at all, until a chillingly cold voice said, "No one is going to do anything right now."

Then they did indeed notice that the figure that had been lying at the base of the tree had not been one of the Maidens of the Hunt, but Beloved herself, who now stood with a knife at Martha Hunter's throat.

From the far side of the massive tree came a dozen Hunters, led by the man Kenneth.

"Let her go, Grandmother Beloved," said Ian, struggling to keep his voice calm. "It's over. The Hunt is done."

Beloved spat on the ground. "The Hunt may be done, but my task is not." The sense of confident command in her voice was terrifying, as if there were no question in her mind that now, at last, she held the outcome in her hands.

"This misbegotten world has very little time left, and I do not mind dying with it if that is what it takes to end the curse of the unicorns. Nor do these men, who are neither traitors nor cowards like you, Ian. There are not enough of you to overcome us. All we need to do is wait — or, if you insist, fight you to a standstill. Either way, it is but minutes before Luster will perish, and with its death throes take every last one of the unicorns." She smiled, a look of ice and venom. "It matters little to me if I die along with you. My grand task will finally be complete."

Far above, unaware of the drama playing out at the base of the tree, Firethroat could feel the convulsions of the Axis Mundi growing worse. It was not just that the terrible pressure had increased. She felt a kind of sickness in the tree that seemed to flow from it directly into her spirit, a dark sense of dread and loss and approaching oblivion that made her fear she might swoon.

"Sister," she said, "our work is nearly finished. We have done what we could. When the tree can stand no longer, we must release it. Once we do, we can fly between worlds. It is not easy, but I have done it. I will show you the way."

"I do not think I will be able to go," replied Graumag, her voice weak and strained.

At the sound of her Flame Sister's words, Firethroat felt a twist of grief. "Graumag, are you all right?"

"I fear not, Sister," hissed the other dragon. "I fear not."

Though the dying world rumbled louder than ever, a dreadful silence gripped the humans and creatures gathered at the base of the tree.

After a moment, Beloved said with casual cruelty, "I wonder how much longer this will take."

Cara glanced at Elihu. His jaw muscles were clenched, his once again beautiful face dark with suppressed rage. She wondered if he was about to launch an attack.

"Let Martha go," pleaded Ian.

Beloved's laugh was cold, mirthless. "After the way you betrayed me, you expect mercy, Ian? You're even more of a fool than I thought. It's a pity that daughter of yours isn't here to share these last minutes. She was the only one I ever really feared, you know. The Whisperer gave me a prophecy long ago that only someone who carried both the blood of the Hunters and the blood of the unicorns could defeat me. I thought the idea was mad the first time I heard it. How could such a thing be, that these bloodlines could merge? Then, slowly, I learned the truth about your daughter's heritage. I can't tell you what a relief it was when she disappeared and it became clear that she was dead."

Amalia and Jacques cried out in grief at these words. As they did, the world shook — and shook again.

THE GATHERED GLORY

* * *

"I can hold no longer," gasped Graumag.

Firethroat loosed her grip on her Flame Sister's front legs. To her horror, the smaller dragon toppled backward. She twisted downward, clawing at the trunk as she did. She tried to cling to it, but her body grew limp.

Firethroat wanted to reach for her, to help, but could not think how. Worse, her own body was still held to the tree by the way the lower part was wrapped with Graumag's around the trunk.

She felt that change as Graumag's coils grew slack, the muscles relaxing, her body unwinding. The smaller dragon groaned, a sound from deep within. Firethroat writhed and slithered, trying to pull herself loose.

Suddenly Graumag's body broke free, the lower part whipping around as it was pulled from the tree.

The bronze dragon made no cry as she fell.

Feng Yuan gasped. "Look!" she cried, pointing upward.

Beloved laughed, as if she could not believe anyone would try such a foolish stunt.

An instant later, Graumag's massive body crashed down between the two groups. The leading bone on her right wing struck three of the Hunters, killing them instantly. A fourth lay on the ground, screaming with pain. Beloved leaped backward, barely avoiding being sliced in half by one of the spines in the dragon's crest. Martha twisted free of her grip.

The impact of the dragon's fall seemed to reawaken the sleeping ground. At once the tremors that had been held at bay began again, so that the ground was as restless here as in the rest of the meadow.

Deep in the soil below, Namza and M'Gama, tangled in the tree's roots, felt their spirits being wrenched apart.

As Cara cried out in horror at the fall of her friend, Ian, Jacques, and Elihu vaulted over the dragon's still and silent body. Ian snatched up Martha. Jacques and Elihu grabbed Beloved and pinned her arms behind her.

The unicorns and Rocky's cove hurried around Graumag's body, but were only in time to see the last of the Hunters escape into the tree.

Kenneth alone remained to defend Beloved. He was swinging his sword at Ian when suddenly he howled and staggered sideways

"It is not good to try to hurt my friends," said Rajiv, who had crawled up behind Kenneth and slashed the tendons in his right knee. As the Hunter cried out in rage and pain the street boy calmly slashed the tendons in the other knee, then scurried away as Kenneth fell.

Elihu thrust Beloved toward Ian. "Hold her fast!" he ordered.

The ancient enemy of the unicorns screamed and writhed as Ian and Jacques grasped her arms and held them tight behind her back. Her eyes blazed and her long white hair lashed out like whips made of moonlight. Ian and Jacques had to close their eyes against its stinging strands.

Without a word, Elihu sprinted toward the tree, then leaped into the gaping wound that Beloved had ripped through its trunk.

He began to chant, calling out in a language that even Cara, with her gift of tongues, could not understand. She knew only that the words he uttered sounded as if they were wrenched from a place deep in his soul and were ancient beyond understanding. She seemed to feel them in her skin.

A strange glow began to emanate from Elihu. His body growing, he stretched upward, extending his hands until he was touching the edges of the tree's wound.

He continued chanting.

Cara gasped as light blossomed around him.

In that moment, the wound created by Beloved began to close, sealing itself from the top down.

"Elihu!" called Cara. "Elihu, the tree is healing. Come out! *Come out!*"

Near her, the new Dimblethum pushed himself to his knees and let out a roar. Cara could not tell if what came from his mouth was a sound of triumph or of loss. Probably both, she decided. Turning to Allura, she asked, "Why doesn't Elihu come out?"

"He cannot," replied the golden-haired woman, her voice thick with pain. "He's feeding his life force into the tree, giving it his power to bring it back to health." She watched for a moment longer, then murmured, "It's not enough. *It's not enough!*"

Cara looked back at the tree. The gap at its base was pulsing, growing wider, diminishing, growing wider again, as if it wanted to close but could not.

Allura lifted the Squijum from her shoulder and placed him on Cara's back. "Stay here and be happy," she said fiercely to the little creature.

Then she sprinted toward the tree.

The Squijum screamed as he watched her go.

Even through the blaze of light surrounding him, Cara could see that Elihu was horrified at Allura's approach. She expected him to cry out to the woman to leave, then realized that he could not stop his chanting. Allura tucked herself behind him, wrapped her arms around his bare chest, held him close, resting her head against his shoulder. The light surrounding them blazed with new intensity.

"She's adding her power to his," murmured Amalia in awe.

Elihu continued to chant as Allura's voice merged with his, twining around it like a vine. The sound was so pure, so beautiful, that Cara longed to listen to it forever.

With a lift of her heart, she realized the world was growing quiet, the ground becoming still and solid once more.

The hole in the tree was closing faster, closing in on Elihu, who had made this world and was giving himself to save it, and on Allura, who was giving herself as well, merging with her loved one in his final act of creation and healing.

"Elihu!" roared the new Dimblethum, staggering to his feet and stretching his paws toward the tree. "Elihu! *Alahim!*"

"Farewell, *alahim!*" cried Elihu.

"Farewell, brother!" cried Allura.

With a final rush, the tree sealed itself around them.

A heartbeat later, the ground ceased its trembling.

Where Beloved's tunnel had been was now only a scar, a tall, wide mark in the once perfect trunk.

The Squijum leaped from Cara's shoulder and raced to the tree. He pressed himself to the bark where the trunk had sealed itself and clung to it, weeping as if his tiny heart would break.

30

FIRE ATTEND THEE

Luster: The Axis Mundi

Crouching beside her sister dragon, Firethroat ignored the babble around them. Beloved and Cara's family were behind Graumag's body, closer to the tree. She did not care.

Several unicorns came forward, across the now peaceful meadow.

"Can you heal her?" asked Firethroat, speaking to them in their own language.

One of the unicorns — it was Cloudmane — stepped forward, knelt beside Graumag's still body, touched it with her horn. Rising, she turned to Firethroat. "We will try, but there is not much life force left. We can heal. But we cannot resurrect."

"Try!" urged the dragon. *"Try!"*

The unicorns did try, six of them at once pressing their horns to Graumag's neck. The dragon's great body flinched and twisted. She uttered a soft moan and attempted to raise her head, but was only able to get it a few inches from the ground before it dropped back again.

The unicorns staggered and fell. Cloudmane managed to gasp, "We did what we could. I am sorry it was not enough."

"You did what you could," agreed Firethroat. She placed her long neck beside Graumag's, so that her own vast head was close. "We did a mighty deed this day," she murmured into her Sky Sister's ear. "We saved the world that has given us shelter these many centuries."

"I'm glad," whispered Graumag, her voice barely audible. "I owed my life to Luster. Now the debt is repaid. Oh, Sky Sister, I will not last much longer. I feel the darkness coming and into it I must go."

"Fire attend thee," whispered Firethroat.

Then she drew back, hissing in astonishment.

Graumag had begun to shrink, her body to transform.

"It hurts!" cried the smaller dragon. "Sister, yet again it hurts!"

Moments later the transformation was finished.

On the ground before Firethroat lay not a dragon, but a beautiful woman, naked save for the flaming red tresses that shielded her body.

31
GENERATIONS

Luster: The Axis Mundi

Oblivious to what was happening with the dragons, Beloved screamed and raged, writhed and twisted, spat and cursed. Yet try as she might, she could not break free of the grip in which Ian and Jacques held her.

Arrayed in front of her were Amalia Flickerfoot, Martha Hunter, and the unicorn known as Silverhoof — three generations of women, in the youngest of whom the blood of Hunters and unicorns had merged.

Of the three, only Martha was in human form. Her voice sharp, she said, "You were wrong, Beloved. Cara is not dead."

Jacques and Amalia cried out in relief at these words. Beloved stopped her ranting and stared at Martha. "What do you mean?"

"She means," said Cara slowly and clearly, "I am not dead, simply transformed."

Her father and grandfather were so startled they nearly lost their grip on Beloved's arms. Without thinking, both men opened their eyes — which had been closed against the miniature whips of Beloved's hair — to gape at her. Fortunately, Beloved herself had gone still when understanding overtook her. Slowly her face twisted in bitterness, as if this were the greatest betrayal of them all. Voice now weak, she said, "Then kill me. Kill me at last, and end this endless pain. You are the only one who can end it, you hellborn child. So do it. Do it now!"

Cara stared at Beloved, who had wrought so much death and destruction. She thought about how the woman had been driven, both by her endless agony and by the treacherous urgings of the Whisperer, who had come from the unicorns themselves. And in that staring, in that moment before the choice must be made, which is the only moment of freedom anyone ever really has, she found herself torn between loathing and compassion.

All attention was now focused on Cara, but she was aware only of Beloved, whose blazing eyes stared back at her with hate and pain and defeat.

Cara took a deep breath. "Hold her tight," she cautioned her father and Jacques. Then, to Beloved, she said, "If I am the only one who can kill you, then perhaps I am also the only one who could heal you."

She glanced back at her mother and her grandmother.

Amalia made a gentle nod. Martha's face was rigid.

Please let me get this right, thought Cara.

As her father and her possible grandfather held Beloved, Cara stepped forward.

It's in her heart, she thought. The idea was frightening, and there was no guide for this, but it seemed that only one thing would work. Extending her neck, she braced her legs, then thrust her horn into Beloved's chest, driving on until she reached the enemy's heart.

No matter how many times she had seen Lightfoot do this, and seen what it had cost him, no matter that she had tried to heal the Dimblethum and felt some flow of energy then, nothing had prepared Cara for the way this healing pulled at her strength and vitality. The sensation was both exhilarating and excruciating, an odd mix of pain and ecstasy. It was too much to bear, and she wanted to pull back, but braced her legs and forced herself to continue.

Beloved's scream when the horn entered her heart seemed to shred the growing dawn. She spasmed, twisting uncontrollably as she tried to pull herself away. Cara, fearing she had made a mistake and was only wounding Beloved further, tried to pull back. She could not; it felt as if Beloved's heart had seized the horn and would not let go. Her knees buckled. Terrified that she would collapse with Beloved still impaled on her horn, Cara tried again to wrench free. But the horn was stuck fast, as if she and her ancestress were locked in some unholy circle of energy.

Then something changed in the energy flow. With a sudden gasp, Beloved cried out one last time. Then she fell back, the bond broken.

Cara, too, staggered backward, then dropped to her side, exhausted. She heard her mother gasp. Lifting her head, she saw that an astonishing look of peace had come over Beloved's face.

"What have you done?" she whispered, her voice filled with wonder. "*What have you done?*"

Even as Beloved spoke these words, age came upon her at last, the age that had been kept at bay during all the centuries of her mad quest to destroy the unicorns.

Her hands grew twisted and gnarled. Her moon-white hair fell limp. Deep lines seamed their way across her once-smooth face. She lifted her fingers, and a look of horror crossed her coarsening features as she saw them shrink and wither. She closed her eyes, then shook her head. In the papery remnant of a voice that was left to her, she murmured, "It's all right. It's all right. At last the pain is gone."

She collapsed to the ground and made a sound that was half sigh, half sob. In a ghastly whisper she said, "Thank you, child, for this relief."

A moment after that she curled and shriveled into

herself until there was nothing but dust where she had lain.

Cara, exhausted in a way she had never imagined possible, lifted her head to her mother. "I killed her!" she wailed. "I only wanted to help, only wanted to heal her. And now she's dead."

Martha Hunter knelt and lifted her daughter's head into her lap.

"It's all right," she whispered, stroking Cara's silken mane. "It's all right, dear one. You did what only you could do. You brought her peace at last."

AFTER THE BATTLE

32

SCARS AND HOPE

Luster

The weeks that followed the healing of the great tree were painful. Luster was badly damaged and had seen more death in the five days of the invasion than in all the centuries that preceded it.

Amalia Flickerfoot established her base in the meadow of the Axis Mundi; she had much to do, and the center of the world seemed the best place from which to do it.

The major problem with this decision was that great rifts still scored the land all around — gaping crevices that made it hard, even dangerous, to approach the tree. On the other hand, this was true all over Luster

— though in time it became clear that the worst of the damage was at the center, and the farther from the tree you went, the less catastrophic was the destruction. This is not to say it was not bad — cliffs had crumbled; forests had fallen; entire valleys had vanished under the debris of shattered mountains.

The first task was to complete the healing of the unicorns who had been injured in the battle. This took much time and energy, for the wounds were deep and numerous.

A tally was made of the unicorns who had not survived; the list was long and painful to read. When their bodies had faded, as is the way of unicorns, Thomas the Tinker collected their horns. He placed them in his cart — the cockatrice was still there, too — and carried them to the Cavern of the Unicorn Chronicles. In later times a special space was made for them, an underground hall of honor, where each horn stands as proud reminder of those who fought to save their world. Their names were inscribed in a scroll that is kept at the front of this room, and once a year, on the anniversary of Beloved's invasion, their names are read aloud in loving memory. Moonheart's is first among them.

They found the bodies of M'Gama and Namza next to the tree, about a quarter of the way around from the scar that marked where Elihu and Allura had closed the wound. At first the unicorns feared that the two magic makers were dead. But careful examination showed that their hearts still beat, their lungs still moved, if only very, very slowly.

The Queen's Council debated long over whether they should try to wake them with a healing. In the end, Amalia Flickerfoot said, "It may well be that they are yet working their magic among the roots of the Axis Mundi." After a consultation with Rocky, she decreed that a shelter should be built above their bodies to keep them safe.

No one, including the Queen, knew if she had made the right decision. Worry over it kept her awake many long nights thereafter.

As for the delvers, without a king and with their ancient home in shambles, they were cast into despair. That something had also changed inside them only added to their confusion.

That internal change, which had come with the death of the Whisperer, was modest. Yet all felt it . . . a kind of easing of the heart and a lessening of long-held anger.

Rumors began to spread that any delver who rode a unicorn would experience a deeper peace. Most scorned the idea, and some thought it was a lie, created by the unicorns to trick them yet again. Even so, almost everyone, even the skeptics, secretly longed to try it.

Because Rocky's cove was the only one that had not succumbed to the panic, and because they knew more than any about what had actually happened in those last terrible hours, the delvers turned to them for guidance.

Which was how Rocky became the new king of Delvharken. This decision was made easier for the delvers by the lines that scored his face from his time in the Stone. Everyone took them to be a sign of great bravery and wisdom on his part.

The kingship was not an easy task to take on, for Gnurflax had left the People of the Stone in chaos and despair, and their underground home was shattered. At first Rocky tried to decline the crown. But his cove convinced him that it was what his teacher would have wanted, and with this he could not argue.

The younger delvers, especially, were happy with the choice. Though they had not dared to speak of it in the days of the old king, many had come to hate and fear Gnurflax.

Taking nicknames became a fad among those who admired their new leader.

Most of the Hunters had fled through the opening in the tree before it was sealed. Even so, dozens remained in Luster. They fell into two categories. First were those who had fled the battle as it turned against them, but had not made it to the tree. These had disappeared into the wilderness, and there was no way of knowing how many there were. Second were those who had fallen in battle, but were only wounded, not dead.

"We'll heal the ones we can," decreed the Queen.

"You will heal the enemy?" replied Feng Yuan, aghast.

"We are healers," replied Amalia Flickerfoot, "and we are not vengeful. But neither are we fools. Once healed, they will be put into the Deep Sleep."

Cara remembered the story of Martin Hunter, who had tracked her grandmother when she was a teenaged girl named Ivy Morris. "Where will you keep them?" she asked.

"Martin Hunter sleeps in a cave attached to Grimwold's Cavern. We'll put the others there and wake them one at a time. They will be given a choice — we will escort them to one of the gates so that they can leave Luster, or they can prove themselves with service and make a life here."

"Most will probably want to return to Earth," said Ian. "However, now that Beloved is gone, some may indeed want to stay. I think it more likely that some of the Hunt maidens will choose to remain. Feng Yuan has told me there are five who did not make it through the tree."

At the Queen's request, Belle and Feng Yuan agreed to work with the maidens to see if they wished to return to Earth or wanted to try to make a home in Luster.

All that remained in that regard was the disposal of the Hunters who had died in battle. It did seem to please Feng Yuan when the Queen ordered that the corpses simply be rolled into the seemingly bottomless crevices.

* * *

Medafil was among the first to be given a healing by the unicorns. Despite his cry of "Gaaah!", once the healing was complete he muttered, "Oh, well, actually that feels pretty good."

The next day he came to Cara and said, "I must be going now."

"Must you?" she asked. "I would rather you would stay."

"I am weary not only in body but in spirit," said the gryphon. "The only remedy of which I can think is to go off by myself for a time and write some poetry. I don't believe I'm up for an epic yet, but I'm pretty sure I can write some pretty spectacular odes."

"Then I shall eagerly wait for you to return and read them to me," said Cara.

"Gaah! I wish you could give me a kiss goodbye, as your grandmother used to do before she returned to her true form. But now you are a unicorn as well. It's hard to keep track of your family, you know."

Cara laughed. "If you think knowing us is confusing, you should try *being* us!"

"I'd rather not, if it's all the same to you, But I do promise I will come back to visit once I feel up to it."

"I will be waiting for you," replied Cara. "I could not have survived this without you, you know."

"Oh . . . Gaaah!" said the gryphon.

Then he spread his mostly-healed wings and wobbled skyward.

* * *

"For your help in our time of need, I thank you, Firethroat," said the Queen. "I know it cost you dearly."

"This was always your world," replied the dragon, "and we know we came as uninvited guests. Yet I would now make claim that Graumag has paid the price for all of our entry."

"Indeed, she has," agreed Amalia, "many times over. And let us now consider it 'our shared world.'" She paused, then added, "I shall mourn that Luster no longer has seven dragons."

Firethroat twitched one nostril, then said, "Actually, it does."

The Queen looked at the dragon in puzzlement. "I do not understand."

"There has always been another. For reasons of our own, we do not speak of him. But there are indeed still seven dragons in Luster." She looked past Amalia as if considering something, then stretched her great wings and said, "I am returning to my cave now. In time there will be a dragonmoot to mourn the loss of Graumag. Our period of grieving is long, so do not expect to hear from me anytime soon." She paused yet again, then added, "It would be wiser not to disturb us for now."

The Queen nodded and said gently, "We will leave you to your sorrow."

* * *

When Arkon presented himself to the Queen, as had been requested, she said to the centaur, "Your help was most timely, Chiron, and our appreciation is enormous. What boon may I grant you in return?"

"We ask only free passage through Luster."

Amalia shook her head sadly. "That you have always had, my new friend. It was not by our command but by the decision of the old Chiron that your people remained in the valley."

Arkon looked startled, but bowed from the waist and said, "May there be new friendship between our peoples."

"In this, Chiron, we are in agreement. You and I and the Delverking are all new to our positions. It is a good time for change."

Two days after the healing of the tree, Rajiv stood in front of Ian and said, "Sahib, you know I am fond of you. But I must work. It is the rule of Luster that for a boy to stay he must earn his place. Sahib Jacques and Sahib Armando say that I may join the Players. They will teach me many things I wish to learn. You have the memsahib and your daughter, though she is a unicorn, which seems to me very strange. So you will not be lonely, even though Sahib Fallon is gone. And we will see each other again, I believe. I have been learning about this Luster you have brought me to. It is a big world, but not so big as all that. It is a good size for a boy to explore. I know our paths will cross again."

"*Namaste,* Rajiv," said Ian, pressing his palms together and bowing to the boy.

"*Namaste,* Sahib Hunter," he replied. Then his lips trembled. Ian knelt and scooped him into his arms.

"I shall miss you, sahib," murmured the boy, flinging his arms around Ian's neck.

"And I you, my partner in adventure!" They stood that way for a moment, both struggling to hold back tears. Rajiv succumbed first. As his tears fell, he gave Ian a last, quick embrace, then slipped free and scampered off to where Armando de la Quintano stood waiting.

Ian was still wiping at his eyes when the boy and the Ringmaster were out of sight.

That Ian and Martha would stay in Luster was not a matter of question, since Cara could not leave. So on the evening of the second day after the healing of the tree, when the first crush of Amalia's duties had eased, Martha Hunter went to speak with her mother.

Their conversation was long and painful, and — as it turned out — only the first of many it would take to heal the breech between them. Not all things can be made better by the touch of a unicorn's horn. Theirs would be a slow healing, but it had begun.

While they were speaking, Cara went to Jacques and said, "Why won't you ask my grandmother if you are truly my grandfather?"

The old man's woebegone face twisted as if trying to smile. "Oh, my dear girl," he murmured. "As long as I do not know, it remains a happy possibility. And knowing would change nothing. In my heart I long ago claimed you as my grandchild, and I love you as ever much as I could whether the bond of blood is there or not. Much is made in this world of the ties of blood, but I tell you truly the heart is stronger than mere blood, and love needs no such link to blossom and be true. I need neither the joy of assurance nor the sorrow of unhappy knowledge that perhaps another took my place in your grandmother's affections. Between your heart and mine, nothing will change."

One week after the healing of the Axis Mundi, Cara stood beside Lightfoot. They were looking out at the meadow that surrounded the tree. Shoulders touching, they spoke mind-to-mind.

"Do you wish you could return to human form?" asked Lightfoot.

"I don't know. I miss having hands." She paused, feeling a pang of sorrow as she remembered how Finder had once told her that hands were the single thing he envied about humans.

"But . . ." prompted Lightfoot, after several moments had passed.

"But I love being a unicorn. I've never felt so free, so powerful." She paused, then asked shyly, "Does it bother you?"

"No! I mean, no — it is fine with me, though it will take some getting used to."

"It will be harder for me to tease you," said Cara. "I'll miss trying to wind flowers in your mane."

"I won't!" said Lightfoot.

She moved away. He shifted to once more press his shoulder against hers. "I was teasing, too," he said gently.

She leaned back against him, but said nothing. She didn't need to.

The sky was growing dark, stars starting to appear. Her mother and father came to join them. Walking behind them were Amalia Flickerfoot and Jacques. Seeing them, the four of them, Cara felt such a sudden surge of warmth and happiness that she had to blink back tears. Looking away, she noticed something that surprised and thrilled her. "Look!" she said, gesturing with her horn. "That rift — it's smaller than it was yesterday!"

All eyes turned to where she was pointing. After a long silence her grandmother said, "The world is starting to heal. I wonder if Luster is doing this on its own or if M'Gama and Namza really are still working among the roots."

Her voice had a wistful note, and Cara knew she was hoping she had made the right decision when chose not to try to wake the magicians.

"Perhaps it's them," said Lightfoot. "Or it might be that Elihu and Allura, even from inside the tree, are working to mend the world he created."

His voice held a kind of wistfulness, too, and Cara knew — not because she was connected to him, but just because she knew him — that he was thinking about his lost friend.

"Perhaps," said Martha, "they are all working together."

"Whatever the cause," said Ian, "it seems Luster may someday be whole again."

How long that healing would take, they did not know. All Cara knew was that the world to which she had given her heart, and for which her beloved Dimblethum had given his life, would survive.

That was enough for now.

With Lightfoot at her side, her mother and father standing nearby, and her grandmother and Jacques close at hand, she felt, for the first time in her life, that she was home.

And it was good.

GRIMWOLD SPEAKS

All these things I know, for it is my job to know them.

Some I know because I was there when they happened.

Others I know because the pieces of the puzzle were brought to me.

All must come to tell me their tales. That is the law of Luster and what it means to be Chronicle Keeper.

In some few places, I have had to guess at what happened or what was being thought. I believe these guesses to be true, or I would not have included them in this chronicle.

So. Now I have written the tale, as was my duty. None that I have ever penned before has given me such sorrow nor yet held the seeds of so much hope for what may come to be.

Only one last thing do I wish to record

before I lay down my pen, and it is this: Every night the Dimblethum, the new Dimblethum, comes to the base of the great tree.

Most nights the Squijum is with him. They annoy each other, but only a little. Mostly they rest in sorrowful peace, side by side, gazing at the tree and longing for the ones they love, the ones who were lost, and will not come again.

As do we all.
As do we all.

Grimwold

Fourth Keeper of the Unicorn Chronicles
The Queen's Forest, Luster

Acknowledgments

To say this series was a long time in the making would be an understatement. When Jean Feiwel at Scholastic invited me to create a unicorn series back in 1991, neither of us could have imagined it would take me nearly two decades to reach the end of the story . . . and, due to the strange ways of publishing, three decades before the full story would be easily available to everyone.

In those years I have been helped enormously by the good eyes and even better ears of many friends, including Daniel Bostick, Cara Coville, Katherine Coville, Kelly Lombardo, Naomi Miller, Tamora Pierce, Michael Stearns, and the late and much-missed Paula Danziger.

I also owe thanks to Pat Brigandi, my editor for the first book, and Zehava Cohn, who guided me through the second. Both helped me shape the world and the story that continued to evolve. For the final volumes the editorial reins were taken up by Dianne Hess and Lisa Meltzer, ably assisted by the wonderful Grace Kendall.

Additionally, my beloved writer's group — Tedd Arnold, MJ Auch, Patience Brewster, Cynthia De Felice, Robin Pulver, Vivian Vande Velde, and Ellen Stoll Walsh — listened patiently in and out of nearly a decade, trying to keep track of the strands of the story even when I would return to it after leaving them hanging for six months or more. Their patience was monumental, and their contributions invaluable. In the last year of writing I added a second writer's group — Ellen Yeomans, MJ Auch, Suzanne Bloom, and

Laurie Halse Anderson — and their input has been likewise invaluable.

For these new, uniform editions I have Jerry Russell to thank for the covers, and Heather Wood not only for the beautiful design work, but for the inspired suggestion that I split up the final two books of the original quartet, which were grotesquely out of proportion to the first two books, to make this seven volume set. Doing so not only balanced out the books, it helped me spot some weaknesses and places that needed repair. Even more important, it let the story unfold in a more organic way. Now I find myself wishing that I had done it this way the first time around! (Well, in truth, I did split up what was originally supposed to be Book 3, since it was heading for an alarming 1000 pages — which is why there was a Book 4 to begin with!)

For the last three books I have also had the invaluable assistance of three wonderful Beta Readers — Jessica Callaway, Robert Gailus, and Elly Klimczak. The books are definitely better as a result of their assistance.

I also want to express not only gratitude but apologies to all the booksellers who spent years dealing with the queries — eager, anxious, sometimes cranky or even furious — about when the next book would be released.

But most of all I must thank the fans who urged me (with varying degrees of patience!) to finish the darn thing. Many who started reading the Chronicles as children grew up while I was trying to write the concluding volume, and I am both chastened and heartened by their emails that let me know they were still eager to read it. If I hadn't been painfully aware that so many people were waiting for this story, I might have given up at any number of points along

ACKNOWLEDGMENTS

the way. So thank YOU, dear fans. It's been a long journey, and I literally could not have done it without you!

Which is not to say there could not be more books about Luster. After all, there are hundreds of scrolls and books in Grimwold's cavern, and they are filled with the tales of the adventures the unicorns and their friends have had across many centuries. So there are certainly stories left to tell, though none quite so epic as this one.

Last, but not least, I should acknowledge my cat, Luna, who is my personal Squijum.

—Bruce Coville

About the Author

Bruce Coville grew up in a rural area around the corner from his grandparents' dairy farm. He considers himself especially lucky to have had a swamp and a forest behind his home.

His writing for children was affected by his own early reading, which included lots of pulp fiction and comic books, but also had a healthy dose of myths and legends — a taste he first developed when his fourth-grade teacher read aloud the story of Odysseus.

He has been reading fantasy ever since and has long dreamed of creating an epic series like The Unicorn Chronicles.

He lives in Syracuse, New York, with his wife, author — illustrator Katherine Coville, and an assortment of cats. You can visit Bruce on the web at www.brucecoville.com.

Made in the USA
Middletown, DE
11 January 2024